P9-AZV-915

It Is Time to Remember

When we were children, we knew everything had its own life and energy. The distance between our world and that which we now call "imaginary" was no further than our closet or back yard. Every blade of grass and every flower had a story to tell. The winds whispered in our ears. Shadows had life, and woods were much more than trees.

In our search for the modern life, we no longer see with a child's eyes, and we scoff and laugh at those who do. In a world of technology and modern conveniences, we have grown insensitive to the nuances of nature. We build boundaries around our lives and shield ourselves from that which we do not understand. Though our lives may seem more safe and secure, they have also lost much wonder and joy.

Enchantment of the Faerie Realm will show you that no world dies. Though the doorways to the enchanted realms may be obscure, there are methods for seeking them out. This book will show you that there are still noble adventures to undertake. It will show you that trees still speak and that caverns do lead to nether realms. It will help you to remember and realize that faeries and elves still dance in nature and in your heart.

Every soul has a purpose, but we can lose sight of it in our involvement with our outer activities and responsibilities. Thus our days often pass with little purpose and even less joy. The faerie realm reminds us to keep joy and creativity alive.

This book will help you rediscover your lost child. It will help you rediscover your own doorways to the realm of faeries. It will help you breathe new joy into your life.

About the Author

Ted Andrews is a full-time author, student and teacher in the metaphysical and spiritual fields. He conducts seminars, symposiums, workshops and lectures throughout the country on many facets of ancient mysticism. Ted works with past-life analysis, auric interpretation, numerology, the Tarot and the Qabala as methods of developing and enhancing inner potential. He is a clairvoyant and a certified spiritualist medium.

Ted is also active in the healing field. He is certified in basic hypnosis and acupressure and is involved in the study and use of herbs as an alternative path. He combines his musical training with more than twenty years of concentrated metaphysical study in the application of "Directed Esoteric Sound" in the healing process. He uses this with other holistic methods of healing, such as "etheric touch," aura and chakra balancing, and crystal and gemstone techniques, in creating individual healing therapies and higher states of consciousness.

Ted Andrews is a contributing author to various metaphysical magazines and has written numerous books, including *Sacred Sounds, How to See and Read the Aura, Dream Alchemy, How to Meet & Work with Spirit Guides,* and *How to Uncover Your Past Lives.*

To Write to the Author

If you wish to contact the author or would like more information about this book, please write to the author in care of Llewellyn Worldwide and we will forward your request. Both the author and publisher appreciate hearing from you and learning of your enjoyment of this book and how it has helped you. Llewellyn Worldwide cannot guarantee that every letter written to the author can be answered, but all will be forwarded. Please write to:

Ted Andrews
c/o Llewellyn Worldwide
P.O. Box 64383-002, St. Paul, MN 55164-0383, U.S.A.

Please enclose a self-addressed, stamped envelope for reply, or $1.00 to cover costs.
If outside the U.S.A., enclose international postal reply coupon.

Free Catalog from Llewellyn

For more than 90 years Llewellyn has brought its readers knowledge in the fields of metaphysics and human potential. Learn about the newest books in spiritual guidance, natural healing, astrology, occult philosophy and more. Enjoy book reviews, new age articles, a calendar of events, plus current advertised products and services. To get your free copy of Llewellyn's *New Worlds of Mind and Spirit*, send your name and address to:

Llewellyn's New Worlds of Mind and Spirit
P.O. Box 64383-002, St. Paul, MN 55164-0383, U.S.A.

Enchantment of the Faerie Realm

Communicate with Nature Spirits & Elementals

Ted Andrews

1994
Llewellyn Publications
St. Paul, Minnesota 55164-0383, U.S.A.

Enchantment of the Faerie Realm. Copyright © 1993 by Ted Andrews. All rights reserved. Printed in the United States of America. No part of this book may be used or reproduced in any manner whatsoever without permission in writing from Llewellyn Publications except in the case of brief quotations embodied in critical articles and reviews.

FIRST EDITION
Fourth Printing, 1994

Cover painting by Hrana Janto
Book design and layout by Trish Finley

Library of Congress Cataloging-in-Publication Data

Andrews, Ted, 1952—
    Enchantment of the faerie realm : communicate with nature
spirits & elements / Ted Andrews.
      p.   cm.
    ISBN 1-87542-002-8
    1. Fairies 2. Spirits. 3. Elves. 4. Nature—Miscellanea.
    I. Title
BF1552.A53   1993
133.1′4′—dc20   92-33148
                                              CIP

Llewellyn Publications
A Division of Llewellyn Worldwide, Ltd.
P.O. 64383, St. Paul, MN 55164-0383

Dedication

To Cara, Sarah, Nicholas and Ryan—
To Teddy, Katie, Babs and Corey—
To everyone whose inner child can still hear
the whispers of enchantment

May your eyes be always open
May your hearts overflow
That which enchants will also protect—
May this you always know

Other Books by Ted Andrews

Simplified Magic
Imagick
The Sacred Power in Your Name
How to See and Read the Aura
How to Heal with Color
How to Uncover Your Past Lives
Dream Alchemy
The Magical Name
Sacred Sounds
How to Meet & Work with Spirit Guides
Magickal Dance
The Occult Christ
Animal Speak

Forthcoming by Ted Andrews

The Healer's Manual

Table of Contents

꧁ꕥ꧂

Introduction

A Faerie Tale*

A man by the name of Brian made his living by cutting rods and making baskets to sell. One year, he was unable to find the right rods to make the quality baskets for which he had come to be known. It was a bad time for Brian, and he didn't know what he should do.

It happened though that there was a glen outside of his town where remarkably fine rods would grow. But nobody dared to cut the rods, for everyone thought it to be a faerie glen. Brian didn't really believe, but he honored it in spite of his disbelief.

Things being difficult, Brian decided he would have to go to the glen anyway. The next morning he arose early. He went out to the glen and before long he had two fine bundles of rods. As he was tying them together and preparing to leave, a fog gathered around him in the glen. Afraid to move, he sat, hoping to wait it out. The fog

---

* Adapted from the Irish tale "The Man Who Had No Tale," found in *Favorite Folktales from Around the World*, edited by Jane Yolen. (New York: Pantheon Books, 1986), pp. 20-23. Permission granted by the Folklore of Ireland Society, Department of Irish Folklore, University College, Ireland.

only grew worse and before long, it had grown so thick and dark that he could not see his hand before his face.

Being afraid to wait any longer, he decided to test his luck and try to find his way home. As he wandered blindly about the glen, he spied a distant light and moved in its direction. Before long he came to a big house. The door was open and a fine light poured out the door and the windows.

As Brian poked his head in the door, he saw an old man and woman sitting next to a fire. They smiled and invited him to sit by the fire. As they talked, the old man asked Brian to tell him a faerie tale.

Brian said, "That is something I have never done in my life. I don't believe in faeries and don't know any faerie tales."

"At least then," said the old woman, "fetch us some water for your keep."

Brian took the bucket and went outside to the well. As he pulled up the water, he accidentally knocked the bucket down the well. As he reached for it, he lost his balance and tumbled after it. He fell further and further, until he landed softly at the bottom. But there was no water at the bottom of this well.

There was a light though, and as he moved to it, he saw an even bigger house. Inside this one were a group of people gathered for a party. A beautiful girl stepped forward and greeted Brian.

"How wonderful that you arrived at this moment, Brian!" she exclaimed. "Several men were about to go in search of a fiddler so that we can all start dancing. And then here you appear—the best fiddler in Ireland!"

"That is something I have never done in my life. I don't know anything about fiddles or how to play them."

"Don't make me a liar," the beautiful girl said, and with a smile she handed Brian a bow and a fiddle.

Brian looked at it and then raised it to his chin. And he began to play. The people laughed and danced, and exclaimed that they had never heard anyone play the fiddle as well as Brian.

Brian smiled, truly amazed at himself. And then a man came through the door, looking for a priest to say mass.

The beautiful girl stood and said, "Well, look no further. Brian here is the best priest in Ireland."

"That is something I have never done in my life. I don't know anything about the mass or being a priest," Brian protested.

"Don't make me a liar," the beautiful girl said.

And before Brian knew it, he was standing on an altar, dressed in the priest vestments. He said the prayers of mass, and the whole congregation exclaimed they had never heard anyone say the prayers better.

As he stepped out of the church, the young girl was waiting for him. Beside her were four men holding a coffin. Three of the men were short and the fourth was so tall, that when they raised the coffin to carry it, it was shaky and lopsided.

One of the men spoke, "We must go get a doctor so we can shorten the legs of the big man to make the carrying level."

"Well, look no further. Brian is the best doctor in Ireland," the young girl exclaimed.

"That is something I have never done in my life. I don't know anything about doctoring," Brian protested yet again.

"Don't make me a liar," the young girl laughed, and she handed Brian a doctor's bag.

Brian took an instrument from the bag and cut off the big man's legs just below the knees. Next he removed a small piece from each of the lower halves to shorten them. Then he stuck the legs back together. The big man was now level with the other three. Brian was astounded by what he had done.

The four men hoisted the coffin and began to carry it off. The young girl followed. She turned and waved for Brian to come along as well. As he hurried to catch up, he did not see an open well along the path. He stepped and fell into it. He tumbled down, falling further and further. And then he landed softly on the grass next to the well outside the home of the old man and woman.

He caught his breath and then filled the water bucket which lay beside him. He took the bucket back to the house. The old man and woman were sitting where he had left them, right next to the fire. It was as if he had never been gone. He set the bucket down and sat down between them.

"Now Brian," said the old man, "can you tell us a faerie tale?"

"I can," Brian answered softly. "I am a man who definitely believes in faeries, and I have a story to tell."

❧

I don't remember a time in my life when I did not see and hear the faeries. As a child some of my strongest memories are of meeting those of the faerie realm through reading simple faerie tales. I was a voracious reader, and anything that had the least bit of fantasy and faerie lore to it could hold me entranced. I remember many nights reading and re-reading certain faerie tales while curled up on my bed or in a chair.

On many occasions I could feel the presence of others, although I could not always see them. Sometimes slight indentations would appear on the bed around me, as if others were settling in to enjoy the stories as well. The first sights were of flickering lights and of a little bearded man lighting a pipe as he leaned against the wall at the head of my bed frame.

He would nod as if tell me to keep on reading, and as I read he seemed to hear my thoughts as words, just as if I were reading aloud to him. Rarely did he speak, but he made his thoughts well known. For the most part, he seemed content to just listen, although his rugged features could change sharply if elves or dwarfs were described within the stories in a manner that was obviously offensive and false. At such times he would snort and look disgusted. Then he would motion with a wave of his hand for me to continue.

Sometimes I did read aloud—using a whispered voice—and on those occasions the lights would grow stronger around me, and there would always seem to be more of a crowd. Much later when I read the story of *Peter Pan*, I was always struck by the similarity of my own scene with that of Peter Pan sitting outside the window and listening as Wendy told her brothers stories of Neverland.

I have seen this little man many times in my life; I consider him my "good luck dwarf." Although this term tends to make him seem like some kind of mascot, he is anything but. He is a wonderful teacher and friend who accepts me as I am. He has shared his magic over the years and opened the mysteries of the faerie realm to me. Whenever I am feeling down or am not sure how things are going, he shows up and the wheels begin moving in my direction. Were it not for him, I would not know that magic and miracles are supposed to happen—that life *is* supposed to work out.

Even today he still comes to visit. As I gathered the material for this book and organized it, he revealed himself as he always does— first with the smell of his pipe and then with his own appearance. He watched me closely, scrutinizing the material I would set forth.

Maybe it's because of this constant watchfulness that I have never doubted the existence of him or others of his realm. Maybe it's because of him that I've kept my imagination alive. Maybe it's because of him that I've always refused to pretend that something I saw was not real. Maybe it's because of him that there's a little bit of the Peter Pan in me that refuses to grow up. And that's not so bad. Growing up may mean putting some of the things of childhood away, but it should never mean putting the *spirit* of childhood away. For when the spirit is put away, the joy and wonder of life are put away as well. Then growing up is nothing more than aging without the growing.

~❦~

Chapter One

Faeries, Elves, Legends and Myths

Nothing fires the imagination as much as the idea of faeries and elves. Unfortunately in our search for the modern life, we have grown insensitive to the nuances of nature. We have built boundaries and we guard ourselves from that which we do not understand.

It has become easy to assume that we know all about the world. After all, we have touched all corners, we have explored the oceans and we have traveled into space. And yet more and more we hear of the search for realms and lands that formed our ancient myths and legends. Humanity is discovering that many of our myths and legends are founded in truth. This is why they still intrigue and fascinate. They touch a primal chord.

Information regarding the ethereal realms is plentiful and found in every part of the world. Whether called Tir Nan Og, Neverland, Eden or Avalon, Hesperides, Elysium, Em Hain or Middle Earth—from the ancient Sumerians to the ancient Greeks—the existence of other realms side by side with ours is an established belief. The information though is not always verifiable. And maybe this is as it should be, for when life loses all of its mystery, it loses all of its vitality as well.

Most of what we do know of the faerie realm comes through stories, tales, poetry and song. Clairvoyants, mystics and seers are also traditional sources. In truth, the awakening to these realms is available to all with a little knowledge, effort and perception. The realm of faeries is only as far away as we allow it to be.

Whether in the form of myths, legends or even faerie tales, such teachings are often not seen for what they truly are. Such allegories reflect greater truths and awarenesses. They are all ever-becoming. They inspire us to the call of the quest—the quest to find our spiritual essence and how best to reverence it within the physical. Such quests are calls to adventure, but they also reflect times of growth and maturing—times of initiation into higher mysteries.

By aligning ourselves with poignant myths and mysteries, our psyche opens. We chase away our boogiemen and we see better in the dark. And that which expands our awareness and perceptions and opens us to greater possibilities can only be of benefit to our lives. By opening ourselves to the possibilities of a faerie realm we invite color, creativity and enchantment back into our lives. And we are blessed by it.

Folklore research reveals that people all over the world believe in rare creatures, both superior and subhuman. Some believe them to be less than gods and more than human. Some believe them to be the spirits of the dead. Others see them as remnants of a race of beings older than humanity. Still others see them as part of an angelic or devic kingdom, working through their own form of evolution.

Throughout this text, we will examine some of the common threads of this magical realm. It is a synthesis only. Though not scientifically verified, it can be personally experienced. This book is a map to your own quest, based upon past writings and my personal explorations. Unless otherwise footnoted, those threads can be discerned more personally by reading and studying the works in the bibliography, by employing the techniques and exercises provided and by studying the folklore associated with this subject.

There are always those who will simply say that this is just the "stuff of fiction." They will say that it is all of the imagination. No scientific data exists. That it is a fool's quest. That it is even the work of the devil.

Humans have a tendency toward smugness. We like to believe we are the highest and the only form of intelligent life. In a universe as vast as that which we live in, such an attitude is arrogant. Just as there are many forces in the universe that we do not yet understand, so there are also dimensions and beings of life that we do not yet recognize or understand.

There will always be those who fear contact with any being or energy outside the physical plane. Usually, the ones most vehement about it also fear contact with other humans outside of their race, sex and religion. What one fears, one will often deny and try to destroy.

In a universe of infinite energies and life forms, anything which expands our awareness and brings joy to our life can only be a benefit. By opening ourselves to the possibility first and then the realization of actuality, we open ourselves to all the wonders of the world waiting to be explored. We open ourselves to the mysteries of life. We have greater opportunity for fulfillment, prosperity and joy within our individual life expressions.

The world still holds an ancient enchantment. It hints of journeys into unseen and unmapped domains. There was a time when the distances between our world and those we consider "imaginary" were no further than a bend in the road. Each cavern and hollow tree was a doorway to another world. Humans recognized life in all things. The streams sang and the winds whispered ancient words into the ears of whoever would listen. Every blade of grass and flower had a tale to tell. In the blink of an eye, one could explore worlds and seek out knowledge that enlightened life. Shadows were not just shadows and woods were not just trees and clouds were not just pretty. There was life and purpose in all things and there was loving interaction between the worlds.

Now we no longer see with a child's or seer's eyes. Instead we laugh and scoff at those who do. Because of this the "blessed ones" have retreated. The abuses we impose on nature and on each other appall them, and though curious about humans, they avoid contact.

However, no world dies completely. Those ancient worlds still exist, though the doorways to them are more obscure. Now we must seek them out. There are still noble adventures to undertake. There are still pots of gold at the end of rainbows, but they must be searched out and won.

I believe in faeries and elves. I believe in trees that speak and caverns that lead to nether realms. I know there are dragons and princesses and wisdom in all things. I have seen angels and devas and beings working with us in all things. My world is full of color and joy and wonder.

Every soul has a purpose, but sometimes we get so lost within our day-to-day activities that our lives pass with little purpose and even less joy. At such times, the soul—through its connection with the divine—attempts to remind us that something is missing. The realm of faeries reminds us to keep joy and creativity alive. It is my hope that through this book and its techniques you will discover your own doorways into this realm and breathe new life into your soul.

Venturing between these worlds often has been described as being fraught with dangers. Even if these realms were only touched briefly, the individual often displayed recognizable characteristics. A restlessness would develop, and the individual's outer life would be dimmed by an inner longing. There would develop a sense of never truly belonging or fitting in, and yet at the same time there would be an inner knowing that somewhere was a place where all things could and would fit. An individual who never slept or slept very little was one who may have set foot across those borders. An individual whose dreams were disturbed by images strange and enticing could also be one touched by faeries.

Often individuals who felt the touch of faeries would lose definition. In many tales, he or she would become a ghost, no longer recognized. The self would become divided. Such instances in these tales often reflect more than what appears on the surface.

As we open to new experiences, we will change, and those closest to us and used to us behaving along certain lines will feel we are no longer recognizable. This is disturbing to others because we are not who we once were. Yes, such experiences can be divisive to the self, but this is most often a good thing. We are not referring to a split personality disorder, but rather we are referring to a division from that old, stale daily ritual of life and the opening to new creative possibilities.

The human essence is a wondrous thing. We are multi-dimensional and we have an energy system that enables us to perceive and respond on many levels—physical and otherwise. Unfortunately, most people become locked into a routine and a life pattern that becomes safe, automatic and has little room for anything out of the ordinary. Most do not want to know about or experience the possibilities of life and energies beyond the obviously physical.

KINGDOMS OF THE DIVINE

This is just one occult construct. There are many dimensions surrounding and interpenetrating the physical plane. With proper exercise and practice, we can learn to use our own energy systems to connect with the beings of these dimensions.

Planes of Existence	Corresponding Subtle Beings
Divine	Gods Goddesses
Monadic	Great Planetary Spirits
Atmic	Devic Lords Masters
Buddhic/Intuitive	Avatars Adepts
Mental	Archangels
Astral	Great Devas Angels
Etheric/Physical	Nature Spirits Elementals

The task for those wishing to open to the faerie realm is to learn to control and direct those higher perceptive capabilities. The human energy system can be controlled to more easily attune to the subtle influences of life, whether it is attuning to the needs of those around us or attuning to those of the faerie realm itself.

The faeries and elves are Mother Nature's children. They are as many sided as nature itself. They vary in size and form and personality. They are not bound to the material precepts we often like to impose. With all of the evidence and all the information that comes through the tales, it is hard—if not impossible—to create a theory that unites them all. They are too diverse, and we must ask ourselves, "Do they *need* to be organized and united?"

Like everything about faeries and elves, the sources of their names are ambiguous. The term "faerie" seems to be derived from the Latin *fatum* or *fate*, in recognition of the skill faeries had in predicting and even controlling human destiny. In France, "feer" referred to the faeries' ability to alter the world that humans saw—to cast a spell over human vision. From "feer" came not only "fee" but the English word "faerie," which encompassed both the art of enchantment and the whole realm in which faeries had their being. "Fairy" and "fay"—other derivatives of the parent word—referred only to individual creatures. For the sake of simplicity, in this work the spelling "faerie" will be used to refer to the whole realm *as well as* to the individual beings of that realm.

A common English term for an individual faerie was "elf"; this came from the Scandinavian and Teutonic traditions and languages. In Scandinavia, the word for "elves" was "alfar," which could reflect any spirit of the mountains, forests and waters. This is quite appropriate since we generally link elves and faeries with all things of the natural world.

There will probably be those who will protest the use of faerie and elf generically to represent those of the nature kingdom, but it is not within the scope of this work to delineate all of the variations and names of these beings. Rather it is an attempt to facilitate the reader's ability to understand and work with them more effectively.

The "good people," as they are sometimes called, held an important position in the world when each tree had a name and every deer was recognized, known and even called by name. They were numerous and very powerful. They played an important role in everyday life. Humans were not the supreme rulers of the physical world. There were many beings in many forms—often equal to humans in cunning, strength and power.

Many worked and lived together with humans. We had more of an instinctual and intuitive connection to all life. They assisted in helping us with crops. They taught us lunar and solar cycles of planting. Eventually though humans quit listening. As the natural world became tamed, the faeries it sheltered became more elusive.

Humans established boundaries and structures. For the faeries

this meant trouble. They are beings to which time was not defined—
nor was nature. As forests were claimed and cleared, so began the
withdrawal of the faeries. Then with the rise of Christianity, belief
and recognition in these other forms of life were discouraged.

Humans cut the links that tied them to the real world of faeries.
In the past, sacrifice, song, praise and prayers were used to keep the
links strong to the forces of nature. Today this is not done. Although
the saying of grace before a meal is a remnant of those ancient rituals, it is not enough. When we lose our connections, things die. And
the same is true of those more ethereal realms. Many of the tales associated with mischievous and cruel pranks by them (i.e. turning
milk sour, etc.) reflect their response to the abuse and neglect of humans toward them and their habitats.

Many doors have closed. Some in the faerie realm have with-
drawn entirely. They left with the woods. Some have adapted to human life. Others are to be found wherever nature is alive and active.
Still others have gone deep underground. There are still house
sprites and brownies, and dark elves are often found in basements
and attics. Every tree and flower still has its spirit. Every woods has
its "lady of the woods." Trolls can be seen occasionally in ditches
and hanging from metal gratings and the underside of bridges.
Where nature is freest and most wild, faeries and elves are most numerous.

Today the faerie realm is not so accessible. The shadow lands
still lie hidden in the countryside, but never are they clearly seen.
Any opening in sea or land may mark the borders of enchantment.
This can be a whirlpool, lake, cavern or well. It may be a bend in the
road or an intersection of two paths. Though the entrances are elusive, they *can* be discovered.

Children, poets, seers and healers often find them without realizing. Those with second sight and humans at peace and in tune
with natural surroundings will have access to these realms and the
beautiful beings within them. The rest of this text will help you pinpoint those doors and provide you with ways to open yourself to the
joys of the faerie realm.

EXPERIENCING THE FAERIE REALM

Although many beings of this realm hide from human contact,
the ability to experience them is accessible to all with a little patience

and persistence. Those of this realm are intrigued by humans and the vitality for life that we can express. They are around more than you might imagine.

As we will see in later chapters, they have many abilities. Although you may not initially see them with physical vision, the places they can be found are very physical and visible. The more time you spend around such places, the greater the opportunity to establish contact.

Initially their presence is translated through the five senses. This may come to you as a scent. You may catch a sparkle out of the corner of the eye. You may find your eyes start to tear a little. You may hear a soft tinkling. The more you pay attention to these perceptions, no matter how slight or imaginary they may seem, the more you will become aware of their presence. (Also, be careful about assuming that that which is imagined is the same as that which is not real. They are *not* synonymous.)

Most techniques for establishing any kind of spirit contact are simple. They depend upon effective meditative abilities. If we are wanting to open to vision, we must learn to shift eye dominance when in this meditative state. This often happens automatically when we use any kind of altered consciousness. The use of visualization, concentration and creative imagination will lead to higher forms of inspiration and a fully conscious perception of the faerie realm.

Of the three, the creative imagination is most important. Its proper development will open the spiritual background of physical life. We begin to see the spiritual essences and energies surrounding and interplaying with the physical world at all times. Energy translated from the supersensible to the sensible realm of physical life must take the form of images for us to begin to work with them. This is true when working with the faerie realm as well. Those of this realm will often dress and appear according to our imagination and expectation.

What we consider imagination is a reality in some form on a level beyond the normal sensory world. With creative imagination we create new awareness and a new relationship in color and form to this world. Meditation helps us to trigger the image-making and perceptive abilities of the mind.

This induces right-brain activity. Through the right hemisphere of the brain we "see" things that may be imaginary—existing only in the mind's eye—or recall things that may be real. We see how things exist in space and how parts go together as a whole. We see that which may be hidden, we understand metaphors, we dream and we have leaps of insight. The intuitive, the subjective, the relational, the holistic, the time-free mode are all processes of the right hemisphere of the brain. The images created by it reflect our sensory information and data—past, present and future. The right hemisphere is a more direct line to deeper levels of the subconscious mind where ancient memories and subtle perceptions are stored.

How do we tell if what we are experiencing is a reflection of our creative imagination or an actual faerie contact? In the beginning, we use the meditative exercises, and we observe ourselves in them, imagining how it would be experienced. What we imagine is very likely a reflection of what we have observed and encountered subconsciously. The subconscious mind is aware of all expressions of energies we encounter, whether we are consciously aware of them or not. Through the meditation we send a message to the subconscious to give us some feedback on what it is experiencing. The subconscious then translates those experiences to us through the images within the meditation scenario.

We open doors through the imagination, and we explore through inspiration. As we stay open to the experience, we will begin to have conscious encounters. We open ourselves to direct faerie perceptions themselves, rather than perceptions of images. We will begin to recognize them tangibly.

Everyone's experience may be slightly different. Some may find more success by working with the flower faeries, and others by working with the elementals. I have no trouble seeing those within trees and bushes, but I must exert concentration to perceive those of the flower realm. Everyone's energy is different, and thus each must find his or her avenue that is easiest to work within. The rest of this book provides exercises and techniques to begin your quest for the faerie realm.

Exercise #1

This exercise will begin to open your thoughts along the possibility of actual faerie encounters. If you can answer "yes" to any of these questions, you have probably experienced the faerie realm and just did not realize it.

1. Have you ever seen a flash of light or sudden quick movement out of the corner of your eye that could not be explained?

2. Have you ever seen flickers of light around your house plants or flowers?

3. When out in nature, have you ever felt as if the woods themselves were watching you?

4. Have you ever walked down the street and the fragrance of a tree or flower hits you strongly? (This is often a signal that you are being greeted. Some people experience this while those they may be walking with do not.)

5. Do you or have you ever felt uncomfortable in your basement, attic or dark areas of the house? (Dark elves often take up residence in such places.)

6. As a child (and maybe even as an adult) did your closet have to be closed before you could feel comfortable enough to go to sleep? Did you ever see, think or believe there was something or someone in your closet? (Again dark elves that take up residence in people's homes will often use the corners of a closet.)

7. Did you ever have or ever see a child with an "imaginary" playmate? (Often they are not imaginary at all, but are members of the faerie realm.)

8. Did you ever observe children when playing and see them talking to themselves—especially when participating in outdoor activities?

9. Do you find that talking to your plants helps them grow?

10. Have you ever walked through an open field and found yourself brushing spider webs from your face? (Spider webs do not form at face-level in open fields. They need something to cling to. Usually in such occurrences, you have been brushed by field faeries.)

11. Did you ever hear music or singing from unidentified sources?

12. Do your dreams often and consistently involve outdoor environments—woods, fields, streams, etc.? (This can often signal a calling by the faeries to you or memories of times in which you encountered them.)

13. Have you ever encountered an old woman while out walking in nature, only to turn around the next moment and find her gone?

14. Have you ever been sitting outside singing or humming softly and seen animals draw closer? (Faeries and elves often take the form of animals and are drawn to storytelling and music, especially when simple and from the heart.)

15. Have you ever found things inexplicably appearing, disappearing or being rearranged in your house?

16. Did you ever find yourself excessively sleepy when camping or on extended nature outings? (The energies of nature spirits can induce altered states, and if sleeping on or near a faerie mound, you may find yourself unusually tired. I call this the "Rip Van Winkle syndrome.")

17. Do you ever dream of strange beasts or dragons?

18. Do you feel upcoming changes in the weather before there are any signs?

19. Are your favorite times of the day dawn and dusk? Favorite times of the year autumn or spring?

Exercise #2

It is always a good idea to re-read some of the old faerie tales. For many people today, their favorite form of literature involves faerie tales, myths, folktales and fantasies. This can indicate that there is a connection and that the faeries and elves are trying to reach out.

Most people had a favorite faerie tale growing up. Go find that story. If you can, purchase a copy of it in the children's section of the bookstore. If you are not sure what the title is, go to the library and leaf through and read some of the faerie tale collections available.

Re-read that story as if it were an invitation to you to enter into the faerie realm. See yourself as the main character—or whatever character to which you were most drawn. This would not have been a favorite faerie tale for you if it did not resonate within you in a very dynamic way. It can be used to help you understand how you can best perceive, work with and harmonize with those of that realm.

As mentioned earlier, many faerie tales hold truths that go deeper than the surface. They reflect patterns that we are likely to encounter within our life, and they often reveal areas where we can best work with those of this wondrous realm.

~❧~

Chapter Two

The Basics of the Faerie World

Before solid boundaries formed in the world, the faeries roamed freely. Though contact with humans was frequent at one time, the land of faeries was always mysterious. It had different rhythms and rules. It had more of a changeable nature, and this often struck fear in the hearts of humans who liked order.

As humans began to instill order and boundaries in the physical world, the borders of the faerielands shifted. The faeries and elves moved from the great forests to the farms of humans. Some employed their curtains of invisibility. In Greece, there are stories of the dryads whose bodies merged with trees. They can still be seen within the folds of leaves and bark, but when the tree dies so does the nymph.

Humans have tried to classify the numerous kinds of beings of nature. Every country had its own names for them. There were the elves of Scandinavia and the trooping faeries of Britain and Ireland. There were the seelies of Scotland. There were the leshiye of Russia, forest faeries known for their mischief and curiosity. From Greece come many tales of water nymphs and sirens. There were divisions within divisions, but throughout the old world, belief was strong, especially among the Celts, Druids and Scandinavians.

This classifying and naming was also a means for humans to gain power. It helped establish boundaries and control over that which had always been indeterminate and indefinable.

In the past, the faeries and elves were usually placed in one of two categories: those belonging to the wild (the peasant level of the faerie realm) and those belonging to the trooping faeries (the aristocracy of the faerie realm). This division is more of a British/Irish division and can be used generically for most of the faerie and elf kingdoms. Other countries had their own classifications. In Scandinavia, for example, there were two classes: the dark elves and the light elves.

The wild faeries and elves are often solitary. There were rare meetings with humans, and the same is even more true today, with less and less land that is truly wild. Today they often serve as guardians over those lands still relatively unimpinged by human civilization. They do have the ability to shape-shift and will often appear as animals. Most of the time though, their presence is evidenced by activities, such as grass bending, depressions appearing in tall weeds or a whispering of leaves when there is no breeze.

The trooping faeries are often considered the descendants of gods. Included in this category is the famous Tuatha De Danaan, the people of the Celtic goddess Danu. They possessed great magic and were skilled in all areas of life.

The trooping faeries had great power, especially in the use of glamour. This is the ability of the faeries to make humans see what they wanted them to see, or even to see nothing when the faeries wished to remain invisible.

Many tales exist about the experiences of humans kidnapped and taken into UFOs and spaceships. They are then subject to strange sights and experiences. When returned, they behave and are treated just as those who claimed to have slipped into the faerie realms. Because the general public today assumes that faeries and fiction are one and the same, the trooping faeries use their glamour to create UFO encounters. After all, in this modern day of sophisticated technology and rational thinking, this illusion is more likely to be accepted. It is more probable than "a kidnapping to faerieland."

The trooping faeries were also considered the handsomest, and there are many accounts of them (and others of their realm) intermarrying with humans. In ancient times, the current of love between humans and the faeries ran deep and strong. It often held a great price, including death, but it also brought a joy that could live for centuries beyond death.

The descendants of these groups and others are still around today, although there is rarely tangible contact. The curtains of invisibility are removed mostly on the whim of the faeries themselves. Still there are ways to recognize them and open to their presence, and it is begun by being humble, gentle and guileless. If you remain open, you will be surprised at the kinds and the numbers you will begin to see.

Although in the past, great listing and identification was attempted, today we classify the faeries along simpler lines. Many refer to them only as devas. This comes from Sanskrit, meaning "to shine." This term applies mostly to those working in and through the forces of nature. More often, those of the faerie realms are grouped according to their level within the angelic hierarchy. This includes archangels, angels, devas, the multitude of faeries, elves and dwarfs and even the elementals at the lower end of the hierarchy. Today they are all often referred to simply as "nature spirits."

Throughout the rest of this text, we will interchange the generic term of "nature spirits" with the terms "faeries" and "elves." Technically, they are *not* the same. There are variations, similarities and differences, but these can be so numerous that it is easy to become confused. This interchange facilitates understanding, and prevents us from becoming entangled in terminologies.

Almost all nature spirits are intrigued by humans, even if they avoid direct contact. Many even require the assistance of humanity to live and evolve. They have as much effect upon us as we have on them, although we rarely recognize it. Unfortunately, as much as they may be intrigued, they are even more disgusted by human behavior. This has added to their increased withdrawal and reluctance to initiate contact.

Not all of the nature spirits are able to withdraw though. Some work for the maintenance of the Earth and its various environments. They do this until a higher degree of evolution is achieved. Because of their level of development and their task in life, they are bound to suffer the consequences of humankind's maltreatment of the environment. Thus a stream that is polluted will affect such beings, poisoning and often disfiguring them. They are bound to the karma and the effects of that pollution.

For this reason alone, though it may demand greater effort, it is important to establish greater understanding, contact and rapport with them.

SIGNS OF FAERIE APPROACH AND PRESENCE

(Also refer to Exercise #1 in Chapter One)

1. A sudden unexplained trembling or whispering of leaves

2. A whirlwind or dust devil

3. The bending of grass blades with no perceptible cause

4. Sudden, unexplained chills and goose flesh when alone in nature

5. The feeling of an insect walking through your hair, when there is none

6. A rippling of the water when not caused by a fish, a breeze or something tangible

7. Extreme silliness and times of uncontrolled laughter

8. An unexplainable loss of time

THE BEST TIMES FOR FAERIE APPROACH

(All of the " 'tween times")

1. Dawn

2. Dusk

3. Noon

4. Midnight

5. Equinoxes and solstices—especially autumn and spring

The " 'tween times" are those which are not distinct or definable—they are in-between. Dawn is neither day nor night, and neither is dusk. Noon is neither morning nor afternoon, and midnight is neither one day nor the next.

In winter nature sleeps. In summer nature blossoms, and the beings of nature are very busy. In autumn and spring, nature is neither asleep nor fully active. Thus the nature spirits are less occupied and more accessible. With practice, you can learn to spot or sense faeries and elves at the edges of woods while driving or walking along the road at dawn and dusk.

THE BEST PLACES FOR FAERIE APPROACH

(All of the " 'tween places")

1. Where streams divide

2. Intersections of roads

3. Beaches and seashores

4. Lakeshores

5. Fences and border hedges

6. Islands

7. Thresholds

8. Bends in the road

9. Stairwells, landings and hallways

10. Any opening in sea or land

11. Glades in woods

12. Tidal pools

Any place in the natural world that is neither one place nor another belongs to the faerie realm. For example, a river bank is neither the river nor the land. It is a shadow land. An island or peninsula is neither part of the land mass nor of the ocean; it is a shadow land.

One of my strongest experiences of " 'tween times and places" occurred on a canoe trip I took to Algonquin Provincial Park in northern Ontario, Canada. The site chosen to camp was on a small island. It was secluded and quiet. There was a raised area that seemed best for setting up the tent. After setting up the tent, I decided to climb in and rest.

Over the next few days, I found I was sleeping fourteen to sixteen hours a day. I would get up, eat and sit next to the water for a little bit, but then I would go back to the tent and sleep. The sleep was deep and filled with colorful scenarios. I had vivid images of great ancient, underground communities. Animals came and spoke with me.

On the second night I was awakened from these dreams by the haunting melodies of loons and the song of wolf howls (though I had been told that wolves were rarely heard at this time of year). All this blessed me with some of the most wonderful dream and sleep experiences I had ever had. And yet, I could not understand *why* I was sleeping so much.

It would not be until I left this spot and headed back that I realized the reasons for what had occurred. In addition to the altered state that nature spirits induce (especially in as wild an area as the one I was in), the island itself (as with all islands) is a natural " 'tween place," and the raised area where I set up my tent was a faerie mound. I had truly experienced the "Rip Van Winkle syndrome." Then on the canoe trip back, I encountered wildlife (ravens, porcupines, river otters, beavers and others) that confirmed for me my having touched the faerie realm and the spirits of nature in a dynamic way.

THE HABITATS OF NATURE SPIRITS

It is believed that faeries and elves cannot be perceived by vulgar eyes. In spite of this, their habitats are uniformly described in most societies. They live everywhere and nowhere. They are always in woodlands and fields, and the traditional concept of them living in hollow oak trees is more fact than fiction. Any opening in sea or land might mark the borders of enchantment: whirlpools, lakes, caverns, wells, tidal pools, etc.

Intersections of any kind are points where the two worlds intersect. They mark points where there may be the thinning of the veils. This is why dusk and dawn are such powerful and magical times. They are the intersections between day and night. Many tales and superstitions exist about avoiding crossroads at these times.

The nature spirits can be found in caves, across rivers, underwater, around lakes, between bushes and within trees. They can be found under human dwellings and even within. They are always found wherever there are manifestations of nature. Faerie mounds are raised areas upon the ground, indicating their underground habitats. Faerie rings are areas of grass, marked with a perimeter of some kind. They are circular rings in the grass.

The pathways and habitats of the nature spirits will again become more recognizable as you begin to expand your own knowledge and perceptions of them. You will also find that certain nature spirits will be easier for you to perceive than others. Some individuals find them easily recognizable in waterways. I have no trouble seeing them in trees and bushes.

Generally distrustful of humans, they are not quick to reveal themselves. Spend as much time in nature as you can. When you do begin to perceive them, it is often as a glimmer or hint just at the edge of your vision. You may see faces in shrubs or flowers, and you may even assume it is just your imagination.

If not seen, spending time out in nature will at least make you more perceptive of their presence in other ways. You may catch a fragrance of a flower or tree out of the blue. Acknowledge it, for you are being greeted.

Often people walking in open fields will brush at their faces as if they have walked through a spider web. In an open field, spider webs cannot form at the level of the face. This is often a sign of field and flower faeries. They are always active in nature areas of flowers, wild or domestic. They are Tinkerbell kinds of beings, and they are especially drawn to children who are playing outdoors.

Rock and stone spirits are also common, more so than what most imagine. The popularity of crystals has drawn new individuals into contact with this group. In every crystal and stone is a deva or nature spirit that works with it. In larger stone formations, the spirits have a great antiquity about them and a great strength. These stone spirits hold many keys to prophecy, magic and knowledge of secret treasures.

Although mostly inhabiting areas of nature, it is not uncommon to find the elves and faeries taking up residence under and in human dwellings—usually these nature spirits like being around homes with children and where there is a lot of activity. Many of the "imaginary" friends that young children have are of this realm.

Those that take up residence in the home can and do assist in the smooth running and protection of the house, but they can also be mischievous—hiding, borrowing and rearranging things in the house. Tradition says such beings should never be explicitly paid—especially with clothing—or they leave forever. This is reflected in the old story of *The Shoemaker and the Elves*.

Occasionally individuals of a group called the dark elves will take up residence in the homes of humans. They prefer dark corners, attics, basements and closets, and they usually only appear at night. They are not dangerous or harmful, although many are put off by their dark features and strong energy. They can stimulate great craftsmanship, and those who are most creative at night might be surprised at the kind of inspirational assistance they are receiving.

Their energy is strong, and because of this, their presence can be felt. And most people have felt their presence more than they realize. While growing up, my mother did the laundry in the basement, and it was interesting to observe the behavior of my brothers and myself when we had to retrieve it from the basement.

The light would be flipped on, but it was never enough. We would walk calmly down the stairs and begin gathering the clothes. Usually by the time they were gathered, the uneasiness could be felt. The eyes would search the shadows and corners. There might be a chill or the hair might rise a little, and then we would bolt up the stairs (on tiptoe, of course, so as to disguise our fears). Then we would pause at the door to calm ourselves and pretend as we walked through the door that it was all casual.

Many people have had these same experiences in their own basements, closets, attics or other areas. Look how many children won't go to sleep unless they have closed the closet door and checked under the bed. Children are so much more perceptive, but in our society, we train them to ignore it or to chalk it up to imagination. Dark elves are solitary, but they are drawn to children and to homes with children.

These kinds of feelings are not just stimulated by superstitious fears. Often these feelings indicate the presence of a dark elf. Their energy affects our senses. It can cause chills and shivers and a definite feeling of uneasiness or of a presence.

The spirits of nature speak to us often without us ever realizing. Have you ever taken a walk and caught the whiff of a pine as you passed the tree? Did you ever catch the fragrance of a flower while those you were walking with did not? Did a tree rustle on a still day as you passed beneath it? Was there a ripple in a pond or creek just as you sat down beside it? Did a bird ever come and sing specifically to you? These are often nature spirits reaching out and speaking to you, and if you acknowledge them and thank them for such greetings (and it can be done mentally), you will find such occurrences increasing.

The spirits of nature are found in all elements of nature: earth, water, air and fire. Their presence and touch is soft and subtle. If you wish to begin your search for the faerie realms, open to the elements of nature that are closest to you. Look around you, because even if you are not aware of them, the likelihood of their presence is great.

The following is a list to assist you in opening to the nature spirits and inviting their presence into your life:

1. Spend time in nature.

2. Meditate while sitting under trees, around lakes, etc.

3. Have plants and flowers inside your house or apartment.

4. Be cognizant of the abuses of nature and do your part to clean it up and reverence it.

5. Involve yourself in some creative activity on a regular basis. You don't have to be expert in it, but enjoyment of any creative activity will draw those of the faerie realm.

6. Leave an area in your yard to grow wild so that the faeries can play freely.

7. Be generous in your dealings with others. (They will often test this, as will be discussed in Chapter Eleven.)

8. Keep the child in you alive.

9. Place an echinite (fossil sea urchin) on your mantelpiece. They were called faerie loaves, made by the faeries. Those who had them would never want for food and always had faerie assistance.

10. Sing often. Nature spirits gather wherever there is song and music.

FAERIE POWERS AND BEHAVIORS

There is more to the faerie realm than we realize. They are not evil as some would believe, but they can be very mischievous. Their energies are also very stimulating, with an ability to induce altered states of consciousness.

Those faeries known as pixies were often blamed for travelers becoming lost. Their energy is so strong that they can confuse the senses, causing a traveler to miss a familiar marker. This intense energy, especially when in their natural surroundings, creates an altered state of consciousness. In this state, the traveler is less likely to notice his or her surroundings. Sometimes travelers are mislead out of sheer mischief. Turning one's coat inside out was believed to counter this dazed effect of the pixies. This act actually forces the mind to pay more conscious attention.

Those of the faerie realm respond to life with feelings, and they have acquired greater natural control of many universal energies. Because they are not inhibited by physical form, they are capable of demonstrating many of these powers. There are, of course, different powers according to the different types of nature spirits. They all vary in their ability to affect humans and human conditions. Almost all faeries and elves have no true means of offense, and so for their defense, they have other abilities. Some of which include:

1. Glamour—
   People see what the faeries want them to see or see nothing when the faeries wish to be invisible.

2. Levitation

3. Invisibility—
   All faeries, elves and nature spirits have the ability to reveal themselves in physical form if they so desire. They will often take the form that the individual expects of them.

4. Shape-shifting—
   Many faeries and elves can show themselves in various forms. They may take human form. They may take the form of an animal. They may shape-shift to become a flower or even a jewel. They often will take the form expected by the human.

5. Ability to bestow good or ill luck

6. Great craftsmanship

7. Great musical abilities

8. Control over weather

9. Keepers to secrets of great healing and other treasures

10. Ability to instill sleep or other altered states

Those of the faerie realm do have a sense of ethics, in spite of the mischievousness often attributed to them. They do have kindly impulses and are well-disposed to those who pay appropriate respect. Among themselves they maintain a standard of loyalty. They rarely take oaths, as nothing is detested so much as a lie. They dislike babblers and those who betray secrets. They also dislike anyone who disrespects nature in any manner—purposely or otherwise.

They hold in great distaste human ambition, slovenliness, infidelity and inconstancy. It has often been believed that they will not show themselves in homes that are unkempt. They are well-known for their amorousness and their ability to stimulate it in humans.

There are certain taboos associated with nature spirit contact. Being careful not to break these is important to those wanting to work with them. To talk about a faerie or a faerie gift in a bad manner will cause them to withdraw. Denying the faerie or faerie gift will also push them away and can result in a temporary string of bad luck. To reveal the presence of a faerie or the reality of a faerie gift without permission or when it is supposed to be a secret is considered a breach of ethics.

But how do we recognize a faerie gift when we receive one? Faeries and elves often show kindness to humans, especially their favorites. They repay acts of kindness to nature through a series of good luck events. The individual may encounter an unexpected source of prosperity. In the spiritualist seance room, an apport (a gift from a spirit) may be given with the aid of elementals which help them to materialize. These may include special stones, shells, flowers, etc. These gifts often have special significance for the individual.

You may find yourself out walking, and you will be greeted by a lovely fragrance. This can be a gift from a flower faerie. You may find a feather in your path. This may be a gift from a sylph to help you connect with them more strongly. You may have someone give you a crystal or stone out of the blue, saying, "I just feel I was supposed to give this to you. I don't know why. It is just yours." Many times the nature spirit of the stone has sent the message to pass it on to you. This can be a wonderful gift from the gnome kingdom. Someone may hug you or compliment you, all as a result of the influence from the undine kingdom.

The nature spirits teach us not to take things for granted. They teach us to appreciate them and to take joy in all things. We should honor such occasions and give thanks for them—regardless of their source, faerie or otherwise. By honoring gifts, we show the faeries and elves that we are open to the gift of their presence.

When we walk around faerie circles and mounds, rather than walking through or over them, we show respect. When we tip our hat or acknowledge a dust devil, we are acknowledging the sylphs. By not cutting down trees or tearing up bushes without permission or checking with those who may be living in them, we honor them. The more effort we make in all these areas, the stronger the message is sent to those of that realm. We are extending invitations. With constancy, they will make their presence known and your relationship will be off to a good start.

THE MOST COMMONLY ASKED QUESTIONS ABOUT FAERIES AND ELVES

What do faeries really look like?

Faeries and elves have a variety of shapes and forms. They range in size from the very diminutive flower faeries to the great forest and mountain devas. They can be larger than the devas of the redwood trees and tinier than a firefly. Their shapes are very fluid and often indefinable. They can be beautiful or grotesque. Many can change their shapes according to their whims. Some often appear in human form. Many take the appearance of what we normally associate with elves and faeries, often though this is done because humans expect it.

The environment in which they live often determines their colors and shapes, as demonstrated by mermen and mermaids with their fish-like tails. Dwarfs living underground are often small and darker in color. Tree spirits will take the size and shades of the individual trees.

Do faeries and elves have families?

They do not have families in the way we think of them. Theirs is more of a communal life in which the entire community or tribe is the "family." There are, of course, many stories of faerie children and parents, but I often think this is more of a human construct to try to define their way of life. They do have a strong sense of unity to others of their realm, whether from their environment or not, unlike humans who generally consider themselves related only by blood.

How intelligent are faeries and elves?

It varies from group to group and individual to individual. Just as every human has his or her own level of intelligence, so do those of the faerie realm. Many are schooled in healing arts, especially in using the tools of nature. Many are also very skilled and knowledgeable about metalworking and are great artificers. Others, such as the elementals, are developing intelligence. They work with simple, repetitive yet essential tasks, such as helping a blade of grass to grow or helping to maintain the human body. Over time, they will evolve and open to greater intelligence.

Many of the faerie realm are known for their great knowledge, wit and wisdom. The most common example is the leprechaun. No one has ever managed to cheat him out of his hidden pot of gold or magic shilling, for he is very old and has seen all of the tricks and deceptions that humans can employ. At the last minute he always finds a way to divert his captor's attention.

Another example are those known as the moss people who often live at the roots or bases of trees. They are stern upholders of the old ways of life. Traditionally they would insist on certain rules before they would ever consider sharing their secret knowledge, especially where to find the blue flower "ache-no-more" (an aid in childbirth). They also have the knowledge to cure most fatal diseases, and they can turn leaves into gold.

Do faeries and elves just exist in Europe or do they inhabit other countries as well?

Faeries and elves are found in every country of the world. Although we often think of them as being the domain of Europe and other areas of the ancient world, they are found wherever nature is found. They take on the personality of the environment and country which they inhabit.

It is also believed, especially in America, that a number of varieties immigrated to this country along with the humans. The faeries and elves had lost much of their free lands in the old world, and there was plenty of wild in America. Faerie beliefs immigrated with the humans as well. This has shaped to a great degree how these beings still often appear when they show themselves.

All countries have their own variations of faerie lore. Sometimes they are adaptations of European tales, and sometimes they are exclusive to one culture.

What is the difference between faeries and those beings that might serve as spirit guides?

Probably the biggest difference is that faeries and elves and other beings of that realm work more intimately with the Earth and all its expressions of life. We may have a faerie being as a guide or spiritual companion, but most of our guides are usually those spirits who have lived in human form at some point.

Nature spirits are usually found in two predominant areas of our life. Faeries and elves work to help reconnect us to the Earth and realize our intimate relationship with it and all life upon it. They assist in awakening a greater joy and expression of creativity in our lives.

Other spirit guides may do this as well, but they will be limited in what they can teach us in these realms. There will also be more of a constancy in their appearance as they work with us. Those of the faerie realm will change and alter as we grow and awaken.

Can those of the faerie realm hurt us?

They cannot hurt us directly. As mentioned earlier, those of this realm have no true means of offense. They can use their abilities to trick. They can be mischievous. Faerie pranks range in intensity. They have been known to sour milk coming straight from the cow, to affect crops and bestow ill luck when offended. It is important not to become superstitious in this.

Faeries are often known for their thefts. They can be the cause of things disappearing around the house. They are also good at rearranging articles and knickknacks.

To the Puritans, interaction with faeries and elves was always suspicious, and they believed that faeries were part of the devil's family. Probably the greatest harm may come from the raised eyebrows you may receive from others if you express a belief or relay personal experiences with them.

Those of this realm are easy to work with and easy to know. If you disrespect them or an aspect of their life (i.e. nature), you may incur some disfavor. On the other hand, in honoring and respecting their homes and their life, you will incur their favor. Apply common sense, and you will find your life enriched.

Can humans and faeries marry?

There is often much disagreement about this aspect. At one time, when the human world and the faerie realm were more intimately intertwined, there was probably a good possibility. There are many stories which speak of humans and faeries marrying—some happily and some tragically. When there are a great number of stories from various sources along the same line, it does deserve closer scrutiny.

Traditionally, human and faerie marriages had clear-cut guidelines that had to be followed if the union was to succeed. These were often more clearly defined for men who would marry faerie women. First, the husband must not question his wife about her life before him; second, he must never strike her; and, third, he must not look upon her at certain times.

There may, in fact, have been a time in which humans and those of the faerie realm could mate, but that time has passed. We can no longer mate in the traditional sense, but we can form very intimate relationships. There are ways to use astral projection or out-of-body experiences to feel the intimacy of such unions that is hinted at in many tales.

I have heard a number of individuals profess over the years that part of the reason they are never satisfied in relationships or can't form them is because in a past life they fell in love with a faerie being, and nothing human can ever bring them that kind of joy. We must be careful about making assumptions like this, as it is often an excuse not to take responsibility in forming appropriate relationships.

Are there humans who may still have faerie blood in them?

This is often a question that arises out of the previous. Some individuals like to believe that they still carry the blood ties of a life in which they were born from a faerie and human marriage. In most cases this is self-delusion, especially for those that believe in reincarnation. Maybe there was a lifetime in which there was a faerie and a human parent, but that lifetime has passed.

Many see their openness to the faerie realm as a result of this. The explanation is much simpler. As we will see in the next chapter, we each have elementals working with the various aspects of our physical and subtle energy. This gives us an innate link to that more ethereal realm. Most people choose to ignore it, and that is fine if it works for the individual. Others, on some level, have recognized it, but they have incorrectly assumed that it is an actual hereditary derivation.

Those who claim to be blood descendants of faerie lords and beings are often trying to make for themselves an illusion of uniqueness from a life they perceive as very ordinary. This does not diminish the validity of the individual's experiences with faeries and elves, but caution should be taken in making such proclamations.

How can working with faeries and elves help us?

First and foremost, it helps us develop a stronger foundation in our reverence to all life on all dimensions. They can stimulate greater joy, and they can help awaken our own creativity—even when we believe we have none.

Different beings of this realm can assist us in different ways. Some of these wondrous beings are schooled in the healing arts and hold the keys to the natural cures for diseases. Some can assist us in developing greater craftsmanship in our life. Some can assist us in communicating with animals.

The skill of the faeries in weaving and spinning is famous. Often these tales are allegories for helping us to spin certain elements into manifestation within our life. Those of this realm can help us weave our lives more productively. By their example of living and working—including the most mundane tasks—with great joy, we can restore our own joy and sense of personal accomplishment.

What most attracts faeries and elves?

Laughter is always an open invitation. Wherever stories are being told, those of this realm will usually gather to listen. Simple and sincere music and song are always attractive to those of this realm.

These joyful spirits will often gather where children play and in any area in which nature is allowed to grow free—even if only a small section within your own back yard. Wherever there is ceremony, joy and color, these beings will be found.

~❧~

Chapter Three

The Elemental Kingdom

The forces of nature are often classified according to one of four kinds of expression—earth, water, air and fire. Operating at the most primal level with these expressions of force in the natural world are beings called "elementals." Those working with the force of earth in the natural world are called gnomes. Those working with the water force are undines. Those working with the air are sylphs and those with the expressions of fire are the salamanders.

There is often confusion regarding the differences between elementals and other nature spirits—the ones more commonly called elves and faeries. Most people link them together as either nature spirits or as elementals, but there is a difference. They are all of the same hierarchy (angelic), but they serve different functions.

Those of the faerie and elf level are more likely to display personality, while the elementals will display a more general characteristic. For example, in one family there may be a particular characteristic or trait that all members of that family have. This may be a tendency to baldness, thinness, a sharp nose, blonde hair, etc. Each person in that family though will display a unique personality, despite the common characteristic.

Elementals are the building blocks of nature. They are close to being true energy and consciousness, and they have not developed enough to truly take on personality. When we are in contact with them, they stimulate strong, definable responses in us. These responses are characterized by and labeled with an elemental designation—earth, water, air and fire.

Each kind of elemental reflects a basic energy pattern of the faerie realm as it builds and manifests in nature. They interweave to create and sustain all matter on Earth. All four kinds of elementals exist in every aspect of nature and in every person. We cannot exist if any of them are missing from our life.

These are not mere labels, symbols or even concepts. They are actual vital forces found within ourselves and within nature. They make up everything that can be perceived by the five senses. In mythology, deities were aligned with specific elemental forces. There were fire gods and goddesses and so it was with all of the elements. (This will be explored further in the following chapters.)

The individual faeries and elves also have an affinity to one or more of these elements and are often found close to its expression in nature. Water sprites and faeries are found near waters, wood elves are found near woods, and so on. This means that the energies of that element are more easily used and expressed by those aligned with it.

We need to learn to work with this level of the angelic hierarchy just as much as we need to know and work with those we call the faeries and elves. In many ways, the elementals are more crucial to our life. We have all heard the phrase "being out of one's element." Without any one of them, we will have imbalance at some level.

The elementals charge and energize us. They provide the fuel we need to feel alive. They work with every aspect of our being—physical, emotional, mental and spiritual. In fact, we have an elemental that is assigned to work with us at each of these levels.

By being around us, these elementals have increased opportunity to develop personality and move higher within their hierarchy. Learning to work with them is a dynamic way of attuning to all the energies of nature and its effects upon us. It facilitates control over our own energy system on all levels (physical and otherwise).

CONDITIONS FOR CONNECTING
WITH NATURE SPIRITS

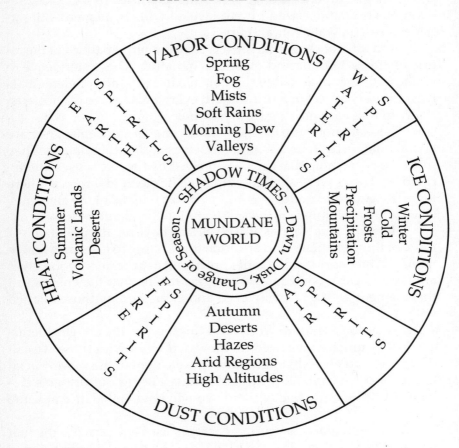

In the chart above we can determine which nature spirits and elementals we can more easily connect with based on the conditions at the time. For example, at a time in which vapor conditions are strong (spring, mists, fogs, etc.) there will be greater facility in connecting with and attuning to both the earth and water nature spirits and elementals. (These are listed on each side of the specific conditions.) We can use this then to re-charge ourselves and our personal elementals accordingly.

Like the faeries and elves, elementals are also four-dimensional. They have nothing to obstruct their movements. Therefore, they move as easily through matter as we do air. They do require some contact with humans for their own evolution.

Overseeing their activity is a higher developed being of that element, traditionally called the king. The archangels oversee the activities of the kings, and the kings oversee the activities of a group of elementals and nature spirits in turn. Everything is hierarchical in the evolutionary scheme.

Element	Elemental Beings	King	Angel
Earth	Gnomes	Ghob	Auriel
Water	Undines	Niksa	Gabriel
Air	Sylphs	Paralda	Raphael
Fire	Salamanders	Djinn	Michael

Gnomes (Earth Elementals)

This is a generic title, and it should not be confused with our usual conception of the gnome often depicted in books, at least not on the elemental level of the faerie kingdom. Their form and shape vary but are "earthy" in nature. They cannot fly, and they can be burned in fire. They grow old in much the same manner as humans.

Various types of entities fall into this general category, each with its own level of consciousness. These beings work and maintain the physical structure of Earth. They help create color in the world and our lives. They assist us in tying into the Earth's energies and in understanding how to use those hidden forces.

The gnomes are needed to build plants, flowers and trees. It is their task to tint them, to make minerals and crystals and to maintain the Earth so that we have a place to grow and evolve. They are beings of great craftsmanship.

The gnomes guard the treasures of the Earth and when attuned to will help humans to find treasures within the Earth or parts of it. This can be anything from finding the hidden treasure or energy of a crystal to finding the gold within one's life.

They work with humans primarily through nature. They give each stone its own individuality—its own energy. They do this with every aspect of nature. Thus every tree, rock and flower has something to teach us.

Gnomes also work to maintain the physical bodies of humans—composition, assimilation of minerals, etc. Without them we could not function in the physical world. One earth elemental is usually assigned to help us throughout our life to maintain our physical vehicles. It is through this intimate connection that they can evolve and become ensouled. They are affected by what we do. If we abuse the body, we abuse the elemental assigned to us.

This elemental helps us to become aware of our physical senses and to develop reliance on them. This personal gnome also assists us with endurance and persistence. It helps us to look out for ourselves, giving us the quality of caution.

Too little connection with our personal gnome and other earth elementals may make us "spaced out." We will have a tendency to ignore the requirements of survival. We may always feel totally out of place and become lost in a world of imagination. There is also a greater likelihood of ignoring the requirements of the human body. We may never look before we leap. All of these indicate a need to get in touch with our personal gnome.

Too much connection with the earth elementals and earth spirits will stimulate narrowness of vision. We will find ourselves being overly practical, cynical and skeptical. Its energies can make us overly cautious and conventional. We may become suspicious and the imagination will be limited.

By attuning to our personal gnome and its energies more directly, we can develop determination and appreciation. We develop an openness to its influence which can assist us in becoming more spontaneously helpful and humble. The gnomes are most easily controlled and directed through cheerful generosity.

Undines (Water Elementals)

This is a classification for those beings associated with the water force and element. Wherever there is a natural source of water, they can be found. All water upon the planet—rain, river, ocean, etc.—has undine activity. They, like the gnomes, are also subject to mortality, but they are more enduring.

Water is the well of life, and these beings are essential to us finding that well within. They are essential to awakening the gifts of empathy, healing and purification.

Many tales have come down to us of various water sprites and spirits, including mermaids. These are a more highly developed level of faerie working with and in the water element. The undines themselves though are usually more primal and not as developed. They often appear female in form, although there are both male and female forms of the more developed water spirits (i.e. mermen and mermaids).

The undines work to maintain the astral body of humans and to awaken and stimulate our feeling nature. They assist in unfolding heightened psychic feelings, as well as emotional ones. Theirs is the energy of creation, birth, intuition and creative imagination. They assist us in absorbing and assimilating life experiences, so that we can use them to the fullest. They help us to see and feel the fullest ecstasy of the creative acts of life, be they sexual, artistic or the performance of a duty with the right emotion.

Undines often make their presence known through our dreams. Dreams of water and sensuality often reflect undine activity and their urging to greater creativity in our life. Working with them can assist us in controlling and directing dream activity, as well as strengthening the astral body for fully conscious, out-of-body experiences.

An undine is also assigned to each of us throughout our life. By learning to attune to it more fully, we open to all of those other nature beings associated with the element of water more fully. Our personal water elemental also helps us to maintain proper functioning of the bodily fluids—blood, lymphatic fluids, etc. Diseases of the blood contaminate them and ties the undine to the karma and the effects of that disease, no matter how unwilling they may be. Abuse of our body abuses them, for once assigned to a human, they can only endure—which is why they are dependent upon us for growth. As we evolve, they will also.

Too little connection with our personal undine or others of the water realm can bring on psychological, emotional and even physical problems. We may manifest difficulties with compassion. We may distrust our intuition, and we can become fanatically fearful of pain. It won't necessarily manifest a lack of sensitivity, but we may appear cold to others. A lack of sympathy, empathy and general passions for life may reflect a need to get in attunement with our personal undine or those water spirits who can affect our feeling nature. Failure to connect with the water elementals on a regular balanced level can increase toxicity levels of the body, for the water won't be flowing and cleansing.

On the other hand, too much connection with water elementals and nature spirits can make us water-logged with emotions and contradictory feelings. Water retention in the body is often a physical signal of this. It can make you self-absorptive with a pronounced imagination and even extreme behaviors. It can make you compulsively passionate. It may generate over-sensuality, overwhelming fear and secretiveness. You may be spending all of your time yearning and emoting, rather than doing, and there will arise a heightened sense of vulnerability.

Through our personal undine, we can get in touch with our feelings and deeper emotions. It can help us awaken to the oneness of creation. It stimulates our nurturing abilities and opens us to the emotional pool where we can find healing compassion and intuition. Because of its fluid nature, the undine is best controlled through firmness.

Sylphs (Air Elementals)

The sylphs are probably more closely in line with our concept of faeries and angels than the other elemental beings. They often work side-by-side with the angels. They are part of the creative force of the air, and it is their work that results in the tiniest of breezes to the mightiest tornadoes.

Air is the source of all life energy. It has been called by many names in many places—prana, chi, ki, etc. It is essential to life. We can go without food and water for extended periods, but we cannot go without air for any great length of time. It is essential to our very existence.

Not all sylphs are restricted to working and living in the air. Many of the sylphs are of high intelligence. Many work for the creation of air and the atmosphere and the proper currents throughout the Earth. When you breathe deeply and notice a sweet freshness in the air, you are acknowledging their work.

Some serve special functions in regards to human activity. Some may work to alleviate pain and suffering, and others may work to stimulate inspiration and creativity. One of their more specialized tasks is to help children who have just passed over. They can also serve as temporary guardian angels, until we open ourselves more fully and draw to us the one who will be the holy guardian angel.

A sylph is assigned to each human throughout life. This sylph helps us to maintain our mental body and our mental development. Thus our thoughts—good or bad—are what most affects them. They help stimulate new knowledge and inspiration. They work to cleanse and uplift our thoughts and our intelligence. They assist us in using the intuitive and the rational together.

On a physical level, our personal sylph works to help us assimilate oxygen from the air we breathe. It works for maintaining all of the functions of air in and around us. Exposure to pollution, smoking, etc. affects their appearance and their effectiveness within our lives.

They often show themselves in human-like form and are very asexual. In fact, they often inspire this in others. In my experience, people with strong sylph activity around them often find that sexuality is not high on a list of priorities, and they often don't understand how it can be so with others. While this can indicate a disconnection with the feeling aspect (the water elemental), we must be careful about making assumptions. The sylphs stimulate different expressions of the creative, sexual drive into other avenues of life, such as work. Care should be taken though not to allow such to become extreme, as we all need a balance of the elements.

Too much connection with air spirits or elementals can make for an overactive mind that must be controlled and guided. It can create a dabbler. It may also show itself through a paralysis of will (too much analyzing). It can also make the nervous system highly activated, instilling a need for frequent change. It may also show itself in various forms of eccentricity. Fanaticism may manifest, along with a general lack of emotion and sensitivity. It may manifest as a detachment from the physical, mundane activities of life.

A deprivation of connection to those of this realm, including our personal sylph, may present itself with impaired perceptions and a lack of common sense. You may find yourself involved continually with actions and feelings and yet not be able to reflect on life. You may demonstrate an inability to gain perspective. It can also cause a weak nervous system. There may be little or no curiosity or imagination.

The sylphs bring inspiration, and they most strongly affect our mental faculties. Learning to connect with your personal sylph will facilitate the assimilation of new knowledge. It can work with us to expand our wisdom. Sylphs in general are good to work with for protection of home and property. Their energy is so strong that they can make possible intruders confused, worried or think twice about entering your environment.

A connection with our personal sylph can open us to the realm of archetypal ideas. It will assist us in coordinating our perceptions and verbalizing them. It can stimulate mental balance, freedom and curiosity. Our personal sylph is controlled through constancy. A consistent life or approach to life is best. This means we make and follow through on commitments with resolution.

Salamanders (Fire Elementals)

Salamanders are found everywhere. No fire is lit without their help. No heat exists without them. Mostly, they are active underground and internally within the body and mind. They are responsible for all lighting, heat, explosions and volcanoes.

These are not to be confused with the lizard-like amphibians. When seen in natural expressions of fire, these elementals often have snake or serpent-like movements within the dancing flames, as if extending out of the fire itself. This was often likened to the slithering movement of the tails of various lizards. This is the only connection to the actual animal.

Salamanders evoke powerful emotional currents in humans. They also stimulate fires of spiritual idealism and perception. Their energy assists in the tearing down of the old and the building of the new, as fire is both destructive and creative in its expression.

Fire elementals work with humans and the world through heat, fire and flame, be it the flame of a candle or the ethereal flames and light of the sun. They can be powerfully effective in healing work in assisting to detoxify the body, especially in critical situations. They must be used carefully at such times, as their energies are dynamic and difficult to control. They are always present when healing is to occur.

Fire elementals work to maintain our spiritual body. They stimulate radiant energy through it, so that it will be passed on to the physical. They stimulate high spirituality, faith and enthusiasm. They awaken spiritual insight over psychic, and they color our perceptions.

We also have a salamander assigned to us throughout our life. It also aids us in the operation of the physical body as well. It assists in circulation and in maintaining proper body temperature. It works with the body's metabolism for greater health. A slow metabolism is often an indication of sluggish salamander activity within the body. A high metabolism is an indication of great salamander activity within the body.

A good connection and relationship with our personal salamander will stimulate vitality and loyalty. It will assist you in becoming more self-willed and assertive. It will inspire strong spiritual currents as well. It will stimulate a new sense of pride and drama for life. Aspirations will remain strong.

Too little connection with your personal fire elemental or any of the spirits of fire may reveal itself through a lack of spiritedness. There will manifest a distrust of life, a lack of faith and a growing sense of pessimism.

Too strong of a connection to this elemental or those of the fire realm may bring on a lack of self-control and sensitivity. There will be a growing sense of restlessness and overactivity that may lead to the a burning the self out. Lack of patience may reflect too strong of an influence from this realm.

Of all the elementals, the salamanders are the most difficult to understand and attune to. They are best controlled through placidness. We can control our inner fires best through tranquil, placid contentment. This means accepting life as it is in the here and now.

Although they are foremost an agent of nature, salamanders have a great love for music and are drawn to it, especially when it is being composed. Their energies are very stirring, and it takes tremendous ability to control and direct them for the most creative results. Anyone who is a composer or poet or in any way works with the creative power of words could do no better than to attune to the fire elementals.

Our personal salamander will help us understand the mysteries of fire. It will help us awaken higher spiritual vision and aspiration. It will stimulate and strengthen the entire auric field so that there is easier attunement to and recognition of the spiritual forces within all aspects of our lives.

ATTUNING TO THE ELEMENTALS

We are more likely to have rapport and resonance with some elementals and nature spirits than others, and it is important to understand and determine this. This will enable us to more easily open the doors to faerie realm perception. There are two simple ways of determining your harmony with the elementals. Your *astrological sign* and your *name* can provide the clues as to which of the elementals you will be able to attune to most easily and consciously.

Every astrological sign is associated with one of the four main elements: earth, water, air or fire. Your birth sign reflects those energies you hope to unfold and develop in this lifetime. The element of that sign indicates a group of the beings from the elemental kingdom. (Refer to the chart on the following page.) These beings of the element will assist you through life in that process if you learn to open to them. This does not mean though that you will not be able to attune and work with the other elementals. It simply indicates that these will probably be the easiest for you to connect with.

The primary concern should be with the element associated with your sun sign. If you wish to examine this even closer and have access to your astrological chart, consider the element of the sign in which your moon at birth appears and the element of the sign which is your ascendant. Sometimes they are different, and sometimes there are duplicate elements. When this occurs there is an even greater need to work with and understand those beings that work with that element.

You may also wish to examine the location of the major planets and the signs in which they appear. Are there a greater number of planets in air signs? Water? Earth? Fire? This can indicate a greater need to learn to work with those elemental beings. The balance of elements is important in handling and utilizing the energies of the elementals effectively within your life.

Element	Vowel	Signs of the Zodiac	Elemental Beings
Fire	I	Aries Leo Sagittarius	Salamanders
Earth	U	Taurus Virgo Capricorn	Gnomes
Air	E	Gemini Libra Aquarius	Sylphs
Water	O	Cancer Scorpio Pisces	Undines
Ether	A	Ether is the substance from which all elements came forth. It overrides and permeates all creation, all signs and all elemental beings.	

A second means of determining which elementals you have the most natural resonance with is through your first name. It is, like the astrological chart, an energy signature, reflecting the play of certain forces within your life. The vowels in your name are the keys to determining with which elementals you are more harmonious.

The primary vowel in your first name indicates which groups of elemental beings you can align with more easily. The primary vowel is the one most strongly pronounced in your name. Other vowels in your name indicate other groups of elementals that are secondary in ease of attunement.

If the astrological element and the name element are the same, it can indicate you have come to double your work with that group of beings and the energies they work with. If they are opposite, they

Vowel	Element	Elemental Beings
A	Ether	All four groups of elementals
I	Fire	Salamanders
E	Air	Sylphs
O	Water	Undines
U	Earth	Gnomes
Y	Fire/Water	Salamanders and Undines

do not cancel each other out. All elements and all elemental beings do work well with each other. It will be your task to learn to harmonize them. Use the chart on the following page to help you determine how the energies of various elementals can work together.

The primary elements of your sun sign and your name provide the fuel you most need to live. The others are important too though, as we cannot exist without all of the elements. If you are missing any of the four elements—even with the combination of the astrological chart and the name analysis—then extra effort must be cultivated to develop and attune to those energies. For example, if you have no water in either your name or your astrological chart, you may have to go out of your way to spend time around watery environments and work more consciously to attune to that element for greater balance in your life.

These primary elements need to be recharged regularly. We need to involve ourselves with the element and in activities associated with those elements if we are to attune more effectively with those beings that work through them.

Combined Elements	Influences
Fire with Fire	Overstimulates impulses and passion; provides much energy for life goals.
Air with Air	Generates excessive mental processes; provides a whirlpool of ideas and expressiveness.
Water with Water	Gives added depth and sensitivity; may demand realistic focus.
Earth with Earth	Causes inertia, materialism, stability; awakens latent talents.
Fire with Earth	Inspires mobility and recognition of boundaries; can stimulate expression or ground passions.
Fire with Air	Strengthens and raises ideals; stimulates inspiration and creativity.
Fire with Water	Teaches alchemical and life-changing processes; awakens rebirth and useful ideas.
Earth with Air	Demonstrates how to stabilize volatile conditions in life; revitalizes.
Earth with Water	Demonstrates the necessity of growth; stabilizes restlessness; awakens compassion.
Air with Water	Renews and refreshes; broadens sympathies and modifies oversensitivity.

The ether element will accentuate and intensify the relationship and activity of every elemental force to which it is applied—for good or bad.

Earth People

Those with this element predominant in their life have the challenge of coping with the stimulating energies of the world. Meeting their material obligations can drain and break links with the basic elemental earth force of their personal gnome. This causes imbalance. Thus it is important for these individuals to regularly recharge and strengthen their connection to the gnome energy by getting their bare feet into the mud and grass. Finding time to be around plants and trees is also very effective.

Water People

Those with this element predominant within their lives need emotional involvement, often of an intense level. If they do not have opportunity to experience regularly the full scope of emotion, the link that ties them with the elemental force of their personal undine will weaken. This in turn will cause health problems on some level. These people need the presence of water and the opportunity to immerse themselves in it to recharge their personal undine and to keep their primal link with it strong. It is a balancing force.

Air People

Those with this as the predominant element need mental stimulation and social involvement. They require channels that offer a free expression of ideas and intellectual freedom to keep their link to the elemental force of their personal sylph strong. If they do not have it, their sylph connection weakens and imbalances begin to manifest. To recharge their primal elemental force and to strengthen their link to their personal sylph, these individuals require clean, thin, electric air on a regular basis. Going to the mountains, away from the humidity, where the air is dry and crisp is essential for them in connecting with those of the air element.

Fire People

Those with this as a predominant element need lots of sun and vigorous activity to recharge and strengthen their links to the primal force of their personal salamander. Work that is physically demanding and active is beneficial for this. These individuals need the outdoors, especially in the summer, so they can store their fire charge to carry them through the winter when the sun energy is not as strong or accessible. Any place where the sun is strong and hot is essential to their health and their ability to connect with their personal salamander and any other being of the fire element.

Once you determine with which elemental kingdom you have the greatest rapport, the process of opening the door to it is simple.

1. Review the information about your elemental, including the king and the archangel for it. We will be using their names to assist us in opening up to our personal elemental.

2. Find a place out in nature that reflects your element. Refer to the section just above to determine which element is best for you. If it is earth, find a secluded spot with rocks and where you can sit (barefooted if possible) with your feet in the mud or in the grass. If it is water, sit by a stream or pond. If it is air, go to the mountains or simply pick a day that is breezy. If it is fire, sit where you can be in the sun.

3. Make sure you will not be disturbed in your spot. Close your eyes, and take several slow, deep breaths. Allow yourself to relax. Start at the top of your head and visualize warm soothing energy pouring down into every part of your body. Take your time with this. The more relaxed you are the easier it will be to attune to the elementals.

4. Now softly tone the archangel's name for your element three times. Do this syllable by syllable.

> Fire – Michael = "Mee – Kah – Ehl"
> Air – Raphael = "Rah – Fah – Ehl"
> Water – Gabriel = "Gah – Bree – Ehl"
> Earth – Auriel = "Ah – Ree – Ehl"

5. Pause and softly tone the name of the king of the element three times. Give each syllable equal emphasis. Know that as you use this name, it is like ringing the doorbell of this being.

Fire – Djinn = "Jihn"
Air – Paralda = "Pah – Rawl – Duh"
Water – Niksa = "Nihk – Suh"
Earth – Ghob = "Ghob" (long o sound)

6. Now softly sing or sound your name outward three times. Follow this with a toning of the primary vowel, the vowel associated with the element. As you inhale, sound it silently. As you exhale, sound it audibly. Do this slowly, deliberately. It acts as a call signal to your own personal elemental.

7. Now sit quietly and extend your senses outward. Feel and sense the energies around you. Do you feel anything upon any area of the body? A tingling? A pressure? A tickling? An itch? What do you hear?

   Now slowly open your eyes and take in the scene before you. Just gaze blankly ahead as if lost in your own thoughts. Don't try to register everything. Do you notice any twinkling? Any glimmers of light out of the corner of your eye or around the ground at your feet? Simply observe now. You can try and analyze it all later. Simply allow yourself to be impressed with how best you can use the energies of this element constructively throughout the day and your life.

   This exercise lets the elementals know you are opening to them. It is an invitation. It tells them you are wanting to work with them more consciously. Used regularly with the other exercises in this book, it will bring you wonderful encounters!

Chapter Four

Nature Spirits
of the Earth

Nature spirits of the earth include beings other than just the elementals. It includes tree and wood elves, flower and field faeries, dwarfs who inhabit rocks and caves and mounds and all of those of the faerie realm who live close to the earth. It includes the leprechauns of Ireland, the brownies of Britain, the kobold of Germany and the nisse of Scandinavia. Most of them are defined by their activities with the earth.

Of all of the earth spirits, probably the dwarfs inspired more tales than any. They are of an ancient race, and they are often considered as old as the rocks they inhabit. The primeval dwarfs were the smiths to the gods, as was reported in the written Icelandic accounts called *The Eddas*. Though often humble and reserved, they are known to champion virtue.

Many stories provided contradictory views of them. They could be potent and pathetic—both at the same time. They could be seen as starving, cold and weary and yet still possess great power. In spite of the contradictions, there are qualities that are universally attributed to them.

1. They have a stunted nature.

2. They have a strong kinship with the Earth.

3. They are often reclusive.

4. There are no women among them. (Because of this they often sculpted progeny from metal and stone, and often they fell in love with mortal women.)

5. They have a great understanding of the primal forces of the Earth.

6. They are often master craftsmen.

7. They are masters of incantation.

8. They hoarded great treasures.

9. They often provided mortals with assistance and gifts, both of which were usually touched with magic.

10. They were the masters of the mundane elements.

     The dwarfs often took on the customs and appearances of their locale. They were the masters of all the elements, and the lowliest of creations upon the Earth are part of dwarf magic. From the coloring of a simple flower to the creation of great caverns, the dwarfs were overseers of much of the natural world.

     At one time there was great intimacy between dwarfs and humans. The rules of this intimacy were always simple and always understood: goodness wrought goodness; cruelty wrought cruelty. Unfortunately, as humans became more "civilized" and "Christianized," the mockery of the dwarfs began. This mockery drove them from human contact.

     Where once they were a unified people, they began to divide and separate. As human mockery increased, some retreated entirely into the Earth, wary of any human contact. Many of these maintained their tribal unity and former majesty, which are still strong today. Others stayed close to humans, remaining loyal to certain

mortal individuals. Some began to sell their services and began to fight among themselves.

This contributed to classifying some of them as "dark elves," "light elves" and even "dusky elves." The dark elves are actually the dwarfs who retreated deep into the Earth. Their skin often reflects the Earth's colors. In general, they refrain from human contact, but occasionally they do take up residence in the homes of humans. As mentioned earlier, their energy is strong, and many people have felt their presence at times in their home.

I relayed earlier a personal story of how my brothers and I acted when we had to retrieve laundry from the basement. The bottom part of the staircase had open steps. Behind them was a small recessed area that you could crawl into if you desired. I used to see eyes peering out from that area through those open steps on occasion. When entering the basement, my brothers and I usually jumped from the landing to the basement floor, bypassing those open steps; and on our return, we would try and take that section of stairs three to four steps at a time, not wanting to linger at all.

Although I didn't know it then, I know now that no harm would have come to us in any way. These dark elves rarely display good nature toward humans—primarily because of what they have suffered at the hands of humans—but they will not harm us. Their energy is intense and easily felt though, and it can be very disconcerting. It can also assist in stimulating one's own inspiration and creativity. That same dark elf from childhood still occasionally shows up, in spite of several moves. It now spends extended time in the attic, which is connected to the room where I do all of my writing.

They are still master craftsmen, and many of them have retained much of their former skills and majesty. They even have the ability to control the weather if they choose.

Those who are known as dusky elves and dwarfs are the most numerous. Whether this is because it is actually so or because they are seen more often is not really known. These individuals take the traditional form and appearance as depicted in many books on gnomes. They are linked to their environment, and thus rarely travel far from their home tree, herb, brook or mound. They are as varied in their sizes and appearances as they are in their tasks.

Those known as the light elves and dwarfs are not traditional at all. In fact, from my own experience, they are not truly part of that same ancient race of dwarfs. They actually fall into a slightly different category which will be covered in Chapter Eleven when we discuss faerie godmothers and patrons.

There are, along with the dwarfs, many kinds of faeries and elves also working with the Earth and its various elements. Most of them that we can encounter work in assisting things to grow. Most still hide themselves from humans, and they will often take the shape of butterflies and birds to do so.

In areas where mounds can be found, care should be taken not to disturb them, as the earth spirits living there control and direct the general fertility of the surrounding land. These beings live inside mounds with all the characteristics of a traditional village life. Learning to attune to them can help you in growing your own crops and plants.

Some people equate the mound folk with trolls. A troll is simply a generic term for a Scandinavian elf and should not be confused with the ugly creatures hanging under bridges and such, as depicted in the tale *The Three Billy Goats Gruff*. They are often tall and thin and have great age and skill. They do prefer underground homes, and a true troll is a master smith and a clever mechanic.

Those trolls that retreated as humans pushed forward still maintain the old skills. Some of them, angry at what they were put through by humans, became troublesome. Some of these still stay close to human environments to evoke fear and create problems, usually mechanical problems with such things as cars and appliances in the home. They can occasionally be seen hanging from metal gratings and the underside of highway overpasses. Pets have a strong sense of their presence, and they will avoid walking over sewer grates and such if a troll is near.

Sometimes the fertility of the land falls under the domain of field faeries and elves, who are its guardians. They resent not being asked to make changes in an environment. They can bring on some tough lessons as a result.

The home in which I now live had been left untended for over a year before it was purchased. The trees, shrubs and grasses were wild in the back yard. Without thinking, I went in and started cutting everything out. The shrubs ended up being extremely difficult to cut down, and they shouldn't have been. I wasn't paying attention to the signals. Since then, it has been a great struggle to make anything grow in that area.

Later, I discovered the reason. I had cut down the homes of many nature spirits, displacing them without their permission. I have had to learn the lesson of how difficult it is and how much energy it takes for nature spirits to make anything grow. It has been difficult rebuilding the trust in the past years. The nature spirits though have returned, and they are even making themselves more known, but it has been an eight-year process. Now before I do any cutting or trimming, I ask their permission and give them advance warning.

Part of the earth spirit realm are the flower faeries. These are always present in areas where there are flowers, wild or domestic. These are the Tinkerbell kinds of beings, and they are always drawn to children, especially those playing outside. (These will be explored more closely in Chapter Eight.)

Rock and stone spirits are also common, more so than what is often imagined. Every stone or crystal has its own faerie or elf. Most of the rock spirits have a great antiquity about them. Great stone devas and angels can be found in major rock formations. These beings hold the keys to prophecy and magic.

Trees not only have their own individual spirit, but they serve as homes to whole communities of faeries, elves and dwarfs. Different faeries and elves attach themselves to different trees. Elves are often born directly into a tree and will take on the energies and characteristics of that particular tree. Tree spirits, usually very affectionate toward humans, will be explored in depth in Chapter Nine, along with the various communities of faeries and elves living in and working with the trees.

Those beings and spirits of the Earth, no matter where they manifest, are crucial to the evolution of humanity. They maintain the Earth and everything upon it so that we have a place to grow and evolve. They are here to assist us in our initiation into the earth element.

Anything of the Earth implies form, shape, weight and a material substance. The initiation of the Earth involves learning how to free ourselves from those limitations. It implies learning all that we can about control of both our physical and our finer bodies of energy (both visible and invisible matter).

Part of what the faeries and elves of the earth element can teach us is that matter is not dead. They can teach us to be practical builders in life. They can teach us how to make things grow properly and in balance. They can teach us about our feminine aspects and how we are connected to the Earth through the things growing upon and within it, just as a child developing in the womb is connected to its mother through an umbilical cord. The faeries and elves of the earth element can teach us to place people before things.

The nature spirits of the Earth teach us practicality and caution. They can teach us the proper expression of ambition and how a proper form of it can be a dynamic force in the universe. There are many benefits to learning to connect with the faeries and elves of the element of earth.

1. We develop greater circumspection.

2. We awaken determination to succeed, along with various means to do so.

3. They help open opportunities for success.

4. They help us to balance greed and manipulation.

5. They can help us to overcome coarse and base expressions of life.

6. They assist us in our timing, helping to bring us back within nature's rhythms where everything can work more easily.

7. They can reveal the treasures of the Earth.

8. They can restore a joy in the experience of mundane activities.

9. They hold the knowledge to using the Earth's resources to cure diseases and to instill prosperity.

10. They awaken a renewed reverence for all expressions of life.

11. They can teach us how to control and use the Earth's forces.

12. They can help us in tapping and using the forces inherent in the human body.

13. They hold the keys to magic.

14. They stimulate artistic energies and craftsmanship.

15. They can teach us to overcome the influences of time.

Exercise #1:
Understanding the Earth Element Through Myths

Many of the ancient myths, legends and tales hold within them the keys to understanding the mysteries of the universe, and the roles of those in the faerie realm in guarding those mysteries. Ancient mysteries were often veiled in tales to provide, for those willing to explore them, opportunities to discover them. The images and characters, although generally treated as fictional, often had a basis in reality.

Specific mythic characters can be used to understand the faerie realm, especially in relationship to the different elements. In their adventures, mythic heroes often encountered beings and creatures that can be thought of as part of this magical realm. For example, the sirens encountered by Odysseus had the same enchanting power many water and wood nymphs had over humans in traditional faerie tales.

Many gods and goddesses of the Earth have demonstrated characteristics and behaviors similar to beings of the faerie realm. An examination of them will provide clues to understanding the forces we are open to by touching this realm. Simply reading about them is a way of opening your perceptions and making yourself more receptive to the more ethereal realms. Some of the more common gods and goddesses associated with the element of earth are:

• Pluto/Hades (Greco-Roman)—god of the underworld

• Pan (Greek)—god of nature

• Graces (Greek)—three sister goddesses who dispense charm and beauty

• Muses (Greek)—nine daughters of Mnemosyne and Zeus who each preside over a different art or science

- Nu Kua (Chinese)—goddess of creation

- Demeter/Ceres (Greco-Roman)—goddess of growth and agriculture

- Dionysus/Bacchus (Greco-Roman)—god of wine

- Cerridwen (Celtic)—goddess of enchantment

- Geb (Egyptian)—god of the earth

- Gaea (Greek)—goddess of the earth

- Rhea (Greek)—great mountain mother

- Mawu (African)—goddess of creation

- Changing Woman (Apache)—goddess of the earth

Exercise #2:
Attuning to Earth Spirits Through Faerie Tales

There are a variety of folk and faerie tales that provide great insight into the character and personality of the many kinds of nature spirits, faeries and elves that are associated with the element of earth. These stories can provide clues as to how to approach and how to work with them.

Reading what has been written about them in story, song and poetry is a means of letting them know you are interested. It opens the doors to allow them to enter more easily.

One of the most dynamic ways of opening to the nature spirits of the earth is by using the tales as a form of meditation. This may seem like a form of fanciful daydreaming, but when applied in the appropriate manner, it becomes a force that opens the doors to this realm. We are simply using the tales as a means for developing a relationship with the faeries, elves and beings of the earth realm. We are building bridges between the outer world of humans and the inner world of faeries. The following folk and faerie tales are effective to use in meditation to open contact with those elves, faeries and nature spirits associated with the element of earth.

- *The Fall of the Earth Giants* (Mexican)

- *The Tale of Persephone and Demeter* (Greek)

- *The Separation of Earth and Sky* (Maori)

- *Tales of Ali Baba* (Arabian)

- *The Three Languages* (German)

- *Snake Magic* (East African/Swahilian)

- *The Man Who Learned the Languages of Animals* (Ghanaian)

- *Rumpelstiltskin* (German)

- *Iubdan, King of the Lepra and the Leprechaun* (Irish)

- *Snow White and Rose Red* (German)

- *A Tale of Tontlawald* (Swedish)

- *The Necklace of Brisings* (Scandinavian)

- *Rip Van Winkle* (United States)

- *Loki, the Dark Elves and the Treasures of the Gods* (Scandinavian)

- *The Tale of Thomas the Rhymer and the Faerie Queen* (British)

- *The Mountain Spirit Rubezahl* (German)

- *The Tale of Orfeo and the Elf Lord* (Greek)

- *Tale of Tam Lin* (British)

- *British Tales of Robin Goodfellow* (British)

- *A Midsummer Night's Dream* (British)

The process for using these or any other tales to open to the faerie realm is simple.

1. This exercise is most effective when performed outside, around things of the Earth (i.e. rocks, trees, grass, etc.). As mentioned in the previous chapter, a place where you can put your feet in the mud or feel the earth in some way with your hands or feet will make this exercise even more effective.

2. Find a time when you will be undisturbed, and re-read the story to familiarize yourself with it.

3. Now close your eyes and relax. Feel yourself connected to the Earth. Place your hands on the ground and feel the earth. Notice the texture, the depth, the strength. Imagine you can feel a slow, deep pulse rising from the heart of the planet. As you do this know you are grounded and protected.

4. With your eyes closed, visualize in your mind that you are standing within a circle of ancient oak trees. Their massive branches and trunk dwarf you. Their bark is twisted and gnarled like the skin of some ancient, giant entity. The upper portions of the roots are exposed, but you know they must extend down into the heart of the Earth itself.

   As you stand beneath them, looking up, they seem to extend forever. You are amazed that trees could be this large. It is as if they form a wall against everything in the outside world. It is as if this inner circle is a point of separation. As you look about you at the giant trees, you are filled with wonder. If ever trees could house gnomes and elves, these surely could.

As you turn slowly around, taking in the sight of the trees, you notice a soft mist forming on the ground. You watch, smiling. It is as if it almost tickles as it forms. Soon the grass is hidden from view, along with the base of those mighty oaks. In a few short moments, the mist closes around you. You are surprised. It seems to have a sweet fragrance, and it leaves a taste of honey upon the lips.

You stand still, watching it swirl around you, and then it begins to descend. As it breaks and dissipates, you find that the scenery has changed. You are no longer in that glen in the midst of that circle of oak trees.

5. At this point you must visualize yourself as the main character in the faerie tale you have chosen. See yourself stepping into the story line and going through all of the activities within the story. Imagine yourself interacting with the people, the faeries and elves and other beings that may be in it.

6. You have entered into the tale itself. You do not have to hold strictly to the story line. Allow for your own creative input. Adjust the story line if it feels right to do so. Use your creative imagination. There is no right or wrong adjustment. If you do not wish to change the story line in any way, then don't. It is important that you be comfortable in this visualization.

7. At the end of the story, visualize the mist rising up and surrounding you again. Then as it dissipates, see yourself back within that glen amidst the circle of trees. Understand that this is a shadow land—a place where the human world and the faerie realm intersect. Know that each time you encounter such intersections, even if only in a meditation, you will strengthen the bridge between you and the faerie realm.

8. Take a slow deep breath, and allow the scene to fade before you. The trees disappear and you feel yourself sitting on that

spot in nature where you first began your meditation. Still keeping your eyes closed, feel the earth again with your hands. Can you feel its pulse now? Does it feel any different than before? Do you notice any fragrances that were not apparent before?

9. Now slowly open your eyes and gaze softly about you. Are there moving shadows? Any glowing spots upon or close to the ground? If there are bushes or trees nearby, can you see any faces within them?

   Don't worry that you may be imagining it. Remember, "imaginary" is not synonymous with "unreal." We could not imagine something unless there were some basis for it on some level of reality. Give thanks to the element of earth and those beings working with it for sharing with you. Remember courtesy operates in all dimensions.

Exercise #3:
Meeting the King of the Gnomes

1. Begin this meditation by finding a time and a place in which you will not be disturbed. This meditation is most effective when performed outdoors around things of the Earth—grass, rocks, trees, etc. A place where you can plant your feet in the mud or be able to feel the grass with your hands is most effective.

2. Close your eyes and take several deep breaths. You may wish to feel and smell the earth around you to help put you into deeper touch with it.

3. Begin a slow, progressive relaxation. Start at the top of your head and begin directing warm, soothing energy to each part of your body, all the way down to your feet. Take your time with this. The more relaxed you are, the greater the effects of the meditation.

4. Now place your hands on the earth itself. Keep your eyes closed through this. Notice how it feels—its temperature, its texture, its solidness. Imagine that you can feel a slow, deep

pulse rising up from the heart of the Earth itself. Feel yourself connected solidly to the Earth and to that inner pulse.

5. Breathe deeply and just relax, allowing the following images to form in your mind:

You see yourself standing in the midst of a circle of ancient oak trees. Their massive branches and trunk dwarf you. Their bark is twisted and gnarled like the skin of some ancient, giant entity. The upper portions of the roots are exposed, but you know they must extend down into the heart of the Earth itself.

As you stand beneath them, looking up, they seem to extend forever. You are amazed that trees could be this large. It is as if they form a wall against everything in the outside world. It is as if this inner circle is a point of separation. As you look about you at the giant trees, you are filled with wonder. If ever trees could house gnomes and elves, these surely could.

The trees are so large that only diffused light enters into their midst. You don't know whether it is day or night. It could be either. In this glen there seems to be a perpetual "in-between" time. It is neither dusk nor dawn, and it never changes.

It is then that you notice a soft mist rising from the ground. It almost tickles as it forms, and soon the grass and your feet are lost in it. You turn around slowly within this circle, observing the shifting mist as it cloaks the base of the trees. As you come back around, through the mist you see a face and figure form within the nearest tree.

Somehow you know that this must be Ghob, the king of the element of earth. You whisper his name, and the mist responds by shifting and dancing, and the figure becomes more clearly defined within the tree.

A second time, you speak the name—this time a little louder and with more confidence. The mist swirls around the base of that tree, and you begin to see the figure move.

Yet a third time you use the name. You send it out strong and clear, and as you do, the mist parts and Ghob steps out from the tree itself.

He is almost as tall as the average human, and he is

dressed like the traditional gnome of folklore. He wears the colors of the earth, greens and browns, and upon his head is a cap. His hair and beard are long, and his features are dark and worn. His face is lined and set, and his eyes study you intensely. He is not sure he should have answered your call.

He notices your uncertainty, and his eyes twinkle, softening his stare—but only for an instant. Then his serious manner returns. He motions for you to sit. He assumes a position across from you. He extends his hand down, and it passes into the earth as if it were merely water. When he withdraws it, he has a handful of soil.

"Every grain of sand and soil is like one of the millions of cells that make up your own body. All of the minerals found within the Earth are also found within you. Thus you are connected to it and it is connected to you. Anything that happens to it will return to you."

He closes his hand around the soil, and as he opens it, you see he has transformed it into a perfect diamond. It shimmers and shines, drawing your eyes to it. He holds it up before you, and as you gaze upon it, images begin to appear and disappear—a moving collage of the abuses of humans upon the Earth.

You see land stripped and left bare to erode from too much mining and greed. You see farmland with soils depleted of minerals through chemicals and overuse. You see rare and precious plants and animals destroyed with little or no thought of long range repercussions upon humanity. Then you see foodstuffs artificially fortified, because natural minerals are rare. You see the greater population anemic and starving. You see images of people dying because the plants that could have healed them are extinct. Your body aches in response to these images.

Then Ghob closes his hand upon the diamond, and then reopens it, revealing the loose sand and soil. Again he closes his fist upon it, and as he opens it, there lies in his palm an exquisite emerald—rich, warm and glowing. It radiates around you, and in your mind you begin to see new images.

You see the life entities of every flower and plant. You see humans working and walking with these entities. You see flower faeries and tree elves. You see water spirits and forest devas. You see humans reverencing life in all its forms. You see those abused lands being restored. You see land that is rich and fertile and you see humans living in balance with it. And you notice that the aches you felt before have disappeared.

"You are connected to the Earth, just as everything upon the Earth is connected to you. What happens to one, happens to the other. Because we are all part of a greater whole, what happens to any one aspect happens to all. This is felt as stress and tension that is often ignored. But it is real. As one person learns to work with the natural world more fully and joyfully, this then influences the whole as well.

As you open to those of my kingdom, you clear the way and facilitate others doing as well. As you develop relationships with those you call the elves and faeries, others will feel the effects. It will be subtle at first, and it may even be ignored, just as the personal effects of the Earth's abuse are often ignored. You will not have to convince them though, for as you open to this realm—on some level of the subconscious—those around you will also know."

Ghob stands and motions for you to do likewise. He closes his fist around the emerald, and with his free hand he takes yours and holds it palm up. He then opens his fist and drops into your palm a perfectly formed crystal ball. As you look at it, you see that it has the markings of the planet Earth.

"This is a sign of my promise to work with you and to help open the Earth and all of its mysteries to you. Do not be fooled by it though, for it carries great responsibility. If you accept it, it is your promise to do your part as well. If you are not yet ready or are not sure, simply leave it upon the ground at your feet when you leave. There it shall remain until you are ready."

Ghob steps back toward the tree out of which he emerged. The mist begins to rise up. It swirls softly and gently. He nods and for a moment you even see a gentle smile and then he is simply a form within the tree. This then fades, until you are standing in the circle of oaks holding the crystal planet.

You think about the responsibility and all that you can do, and you make your decision. As you do the image of the glen within this ancient circle of oaks begins to fade and you find yourself back where you started—at the beginning of your meditation.

~❧~

Excerpt From My Personal Journal

There is an area behind my home that has grown wild with trees and weeds. It has been very important to my home and its balance, as it serves to separate and block the view of an apartment complex that would otherwise look down into my back yard. As I began this chapter after my morning meditation, I heard the sound of large machinery.

I looked out my back window and saw a power shovel beginning to rip up the earth and all that grew in that area that separated me from the apartments. With each gouging of the earth I could hear soft cries and anger coming from those beings who lived within and beneath the trees.

When I went out to investigate, I was informed that the city had ordered the owners to clear it all out. The owners, although nice, were very casual about the whole thing. To them it was going to be a simple task of gutting and then replanting with shrub growth. I returned home and went into meditation for those earth beings living in that area. I opened an invitation for them to come into my yard if necessary.

I came out of my meditation with a distinct feeling that things were going to be unusual over the next few days. As I watched the events unfold, while I compiled and worked on this chapter, the owners of the apartments had more and more difficulty clearing out the area. The power shovel would stop working, they had to dig with their own hands more than they expected and there were little interruptions off and on over the next few days. The weather became scorching and humid, and the dust just hung in the air around them as they worked.

I thought that all this was interesting, but I was not going to attach any more significance to it than necessary at this point. I was in for a surprise though as I began to work on the next chapter . . .

(continued at the end of Chapter Five)

Chapter Five

Water Sprites, Spirits and Nymphs

Water is the creative element of life. Many tales and myths exist about how all life came forth from the spiritual waters. It has long been a symbol of the womb and creation. In Babylonian cosmology, the gods mothered by Tiamat were brought forth from the waters of life. In Scandinavian lore, the sea goddess, Ran, and her male counterpart, Aegir, had nine giant daughters—the waves.

Water is both creative and destructive, a source of life and death. From the amniotic fluids of the prenatal experience to the nourishment it provides throughout life, it is essential to our existence. It is a primary element within the human body, coursing through our veins.

On the other hand, death is often described as a crossing of the waters. In Greek mythology, the underworld is only reached by crossing the river Styx. Many of the world's myths attest to the destructive aspect of water, symbolized by storms and floods.

Water is purifying, and it has rhythm and movement. It represents time and change. Crossing any water was often seen as a change in consciousness and even an initiation.

One such initiation associated with water is baptism. A true ritual baptism in water though is not the dedication ceremony we use today. It was an act prepared for in a meticulous manner, so that when finally enacted, it would loosen the etheric web around the physical body and open one to true spiritual sight. It had a regenerating force that actually made one twice-born. The world was now able to be seen in its true light. The spiritual forces operating through and around everything in the physical become as clear to sight as those of the physical realm.

All the waters of life were considered mysterious. The great oceans and seas were older than anyone knew. They always changed, and yet they were always the same. Civilizations could come and go, but the great seas were always there. From the oceans and the great seas we get life-sustaining foods, and yet many individuals have lost their lives to its depths. Water was always beautiful, always shifting with no beginning and no end.

In more ancient times, the magic of water had no bounds. It could estrange you from that which makes you human, or it could bestow wisdom and spiritual sight. It could cure diseases, and it could even restore youth. In the Celtic tradition there is the Well of the World which could restore life to dead men. In the Arthurian sagas of the Celtic tradition, the Lady of the Lake gave to Arthur the sword Excalibur.

Water has a life of its own. It is a world in which many fantastic creatures and beings exist. These beings are still found within the water kingdoms, and they are not limited to only the undines. Water sprites, spirits and nymphs can be found. Mermaids and mermen occasionally reveal themselves. The water faeries and those beings often thought of as sea gods and goddesses are more fact than fiction. "The American Indians believe that the waters of lakes, rivers, and oceans are inhabited by a mysterious people, the 'Water Indians'."*

Wherever there is a natural source of water, the water spirits can be found. Tiny water faeries can be seen flowing in the sprays of waterfalls. Water sprites can be seen riding the crests of waves in the oceans or on the backs of sea creatures. They can be seen dancing on the surface of bay and shore waters. Mermaids can occasionally be

---

* Manly P. Hall, *The Secret Teachings of All Ages*. (Los Angeles, CA: Philosophical Research Society, Inc., 1977), p. 85.

seen bobbing on the surface of the ocean.

The water faeries of streams and lakes are not as numerous as those of the great oceans and rivers, but they can still be found. In Germany the sprites of lakes and streams are called nixies and stories are still surfacing of human encounters with them. Freshwater ponds are often a wonderful source to discover water faeries.

There are qualities that are universally attributed to most water spirits and faeries.

1. Beauty is their keynote. This beauty is often reflected through feminine forms. This does not mean that there are no male water spirits, as there are mermen and such. Water though is so universally and archetypically feminine, that this may be the most ideal or easiest form for them to appear.

2. They communicate through our emotions.

3. They are generally sweet and gentle.

    There have been many stories of beautiful water nymphs and mermaids who seduce and lead men to their doom or death (i.e. the sirens of ancient Greece with their haunting songs to sailors). Although many of these tales are superstitious, often they are symbolic of the change occurring within the mind and consciousness of one who encounters such a wondrous realm. They can never be the same again, and to many this may have seemed as if they lost their souls or died. Such accounts may reflect that for the first time in their life they caught a true glimpse of their souls. There are many psychological and spiritual interpretations for these associations with doom and death.

4. A fluidness is very characteristic of most. They can present themselves in the most enticing, seductive and appealing forms. They can also take the form of sea creatures (i.e. seals, dolphins, turtles, etc.). Many shore creatures share their magic and serve as a bridge to humans (i.e. turtles, lizards, frogs, etc.).

5. They are generally and genuinely fond of humans, although they are hesitant to reveal themselves.

6. They have a special love of flowers and plants. An ideal way to invite their presence is by gently tossing flower blossoms onto the surface of a pond, stream or other water source.

   If you have access to a freshwater pond, go to it some morning at dawn or dusk, when there is no breeze. Toss the flower blossoms out a few feet from the shore and watch. Within a few minutes, the water will begin to ripple around the blossoms as the water sprites gather.

   Placing bouquets at the edge of the stream or pond can draw a water nymph or even the guardian of the waters into sight.

7. They belong to or are generally confined to their water source. They do have some freedom and can leave it for varying lengths of time, but they almost always stay very close to their home waters.

8. They have a great love for music, and they are often very beautiful singers.

9. They can bestow magical gifts and treasures, including healing and protection. They are skilled in enchantment.

10. They inspire love, inspiration, creative imagination, intuition and clairvoyance.

There is a difference between water elementals and other water faeries and spirits, but it is in degree of evolution. We must remember that all water is *one*—whether in a pot, stream, lake or sea. Thus all water spirits are connected.

Most water spirits replenish our energy. They have an abundance of energy themselves, and it is usually of a healing nature. This is why going to the seashore has such recuperative power.

Different water spirits are found in different locations. Although usually found close to their water source, they are not limited to it. Whenever I visit the ocean, I like to get up early and walk the beach, meditate, commune and play with the water sprites riding on the early morning waves. On one occasion a number of years back, I was being overly playful. I walked along the edge of the water, and as the waves came in, I quickly danced out of the way. It was my way of playing tag with the water sprites. When the waves didn't catch me, I would laugh and sing out, "Nyah, nyah, nyah!"

After the third day of this, I returned to my dwelling to find a necklace missing. It held a medallion that I had had since childhood. I was sure where I put it before leaving for the beach, as I always took great care because of its specialness. I turned the house upside-down looking for it, with no success. I went back to the beach, thinking maybe I had worn it there without realizing. I retraced my steps, but again with no success. I never found it at all, and I returned home without it.

Six months later, when I was back home, I put on a pair of pants that I had not worn in about a year. As I put my hands in the pockets to straighten them out, I discovered my necklace with the medallion. I then heard a laugh, and a chorus of "nyah, nyah, nyah!" I spun around, but there was no one near me. I understood then that the water sprites were not confined solely to their watery element. They had more freedom than I knew, and they had more power than I knew. This was their way of tagging me back, since I had teased them about not being able to do so at the ocean.

Spirits of freshwater areas are usually more delicate in nature and appearance, but we must be careful about making assumptions along this line. For example, the mermaids are the mistresses of the oceans. They protect the sea animals and can bestow gifts upon humans—particularly great medical knowledge. They also can take human form for short periods of time. They have great beauty.

Today, many believe that those sailors who reported seeing mermaids were actually only seeing manatees (sea cows). Having dived with the manatee, I know this could not be. No matter how long an individual has been at sea, there is no way he could mistake a manatee for a beautiful mermaid. There is the possibility though that the mermaid, upon being spied, may have assumed the form of a manatee or some other sea creature.

There are also mermen. They are usually of great age. These male counterparts also often visit the surface, but they rarely interact with humans. The traditional belief is that they have great control over the weather at sea.

The selkies of the Shetland Islands and Iceland were water spirits who took the form of gray seals. At night, they would come ashore and shed their seal skins, walking and dancing in the moonlight as men and women. The female selkies were very beautiful

and desirous. The male selkies were very amorous. Women who wished to have children would cry seven tears into the water to draw out a selkie lover from its depths. After mating, they return to the oceans.

Often the river women and freshwater spirits and nymphs take the temperament reflected by the water in which they live. Some water sprites and spirits are considered devious. The kelpies of Scotland would often take the form of a young horse and lure people onto its back for a ride. It would then rush into a deep pool to drown the rider. Most water spirits, however, adjust their behavior and manner to the humans they encounter. If treated with courtesy and honesty, they return the same courtesy and honesty.

Water sprites and spirits vary in size and form. They can be as tiny as a droplet of water or encompass the entire water source. They usually appear youthful and young, but they do not stay in one form for too long a time. Those freshwater nymphs known as nixies in Germany could also take beautiful human form or, similar to mermaids, half-human and half-fish. As humans, they still can be recognized by a sopping wet bit of clothing.

There are spirits of pools and wells. These also take human form. They are beautiful, enticing and seductive, and their touch is known to bring both great delight and sorrow. This sorrow arises from the longing that occurs when they leave.

There is always at least one being who serves as the guardian to the water source. Sometimes a whole group may serve as guardians, and it is not unusual to find groups of water sprites, spirits and nymphs always together. Remember, all water is connected and this implies relationship. Those of this realm are rarely solitary beings, and unless they know you and are very comfortable with you, you will rarely encounter them alone.

Water has been the most traveled route into the faerie realm. Water links us to the astral dimension where these beings operate more actively, although they are quite capable of moving from that realm to the physical and back again. The borderlands to the various water sources are where encounters with those of this realm is most accessible.

The edges of territory are considered unsafe areas. The points where land meets water are intersections of worlds, doorways by which those of the water realm can enter the physical. Islands, beaches, lakeshores, riverbanks, and the edges of wells are magical points where the mortal world intersects with the faerie realm. It was considered foolhardy to sleep or rest near brooks and the edges of streams. It was likely that you would fall under the enchantments of a water nymph that inhabited or guarded the waters.

Natural ponds, wells and pools are also open doorways and thus very magical. In the Sumerian tale of Gilgamesh, there is a description of an enchanted pool that lies in the ocean floor itself—water within water. In this pool grows a flower that is supposed to preserve human life.

Pools of water after a rain can provide temporary doorways into the faerie realm. There are many magical uses for them. They can provide windows that enable you to look into the faerie realm. Growing up, our yard sported a tree stump that was hollowed down about six inches from the top. After a good hard rain, water would accumulate in that hollowed out area. It acted like a magic mirror, reflecting beautiful faces and scenes of the faerie realm. My grandfather was the one to point this out, telling me to go look inside and never saying why. He would just smile and walk away.

Rainwater captured in a dark bowl or cauldron or even a puddle will do the same thing. By setting a bowl out in the rain or by digging a small rain hole in your yard, you are extending an invitation to those of this realm. Putting a small hole near, but not directly under, a tree is an effective way of creating a window or doorway. When it fills with rainwater, you have an intersection of two worlds.

The steps for seeing through the window are simple.

1. Find a position near it, where you will be undisturbed and be able to look into it.

2. Close your eyes, relax and do a brief (three to five minutes) meditation to harmonize yourself with nature.

3. Make several passes over your watery doorway with your left hand. This imparts sensitivity to the water and serves a gesture of invitation.

4. Be patient and concentrate when gazing into the water. Do not stare intensely. Allow your gaze to be soft and half-focused, as if staring blankly as in daydreaming.

5. Initially, the phenomena will vary. You may see just a fogginess, like clouds passing by. This is positive. It means the door is open. Eventually, colors, images, faces and entire scenes will come. Each time you use this rain pool or bowl, the visions of the faerie realm will increase. Those of this realm will see this pool as a doorway created especially for them.

Tidal pools are extremely magical spots. A tidal pool is water separated from the sea. Because of this, it is a doorway by which water spirits of the faerie realm enter and exit the mortal world. It is also a point in which mortals may leave the physical world to enter the watery realm of faeries. It is also a window by which we can observe this realm.

Shore creatures often share the magic and protection of the water spirits. Sometimes they are signs that such are near. These shore creatures may be turtles, lizards, frogs, seals, otters, cranes, gulls, etc. Sometimes the water nymphs will use a shore creature's form to study humans closer, and sometimes they use them to send messages to humans.

In Japan, there is a story—sometimes referred to as *The Crane and the Turtle*—of a man by the name of Urashima. This man encounters a group of boys abusing a large sea turtle that had been unable to get back to the sea with the tide. He chases the boys off and helps the turtle back to the water. Instead of swimming away the turtle remained, raised its head and thanked Urashima for his kindness.

As a gift, he took Urashima on his back to the place beneath the waters to the home of the sea lord. There Urashima fell in love with the sea lord's daughter. Soon, he longed for his old home and his family, and when he begged to return, he was given a box covered with jewels. He was told by the sea lord's daughter that as long as he kept the box and did not open it, she would serve as his guardian on land. The turtle carried him back to the beach.

Upon his return, he discovered many centuries had passed in the time he was gone, and so he was alone in the world of humans. He cried, and then examined the jeweled box. He decided there was no reason not to open it now and he did. As he opened it, sea mist rose up, revealing a feather. The mist enveloped him, and the feather clung to him. And in an instant, where once stood Urashima, there now stood a beautiful white crane, the bird of longevity.

Anything of the water implies connection to fluidness, emotions and the feminine aspects of life. Through the water spirits we can open more fully to the water initiation. This means we learn to use our emotional forces more appropriately. Through them we can learn to develop intuition and creative imagination. We open ourselves to healing and the development of our psychic natures. All water spirits can teach us about our inner feelings. In learning to connect with them, we can gain many benefits.

1. We develop our psychic nature through contact with them.

2. We learn to be more nurturing.

3. They show us how to develop greater resourcefulness.

4. They teach us about healing.

5. They help us overcome fears of confinement.

6. They assist us in developing flexibility.

7. They stimulate our romantic nature.

8. They awaken compassion and sensitivity.

9. They stimulate artistic inspiration.

10. They helps us to deal with exaggerated emotions.

11. They help us develop greater sensuality.

12. They awaken the creative imagination.

Exercise #1:
Understanding the Water Element Through Myths

There are mythic figures and beings who reflect the energies of the watery element and what it can stimulate. Many of these figures demonstrate characteristics and behaviors similar to those of the faerie realm. An examination of them provides clues to understanding the forces we open to through the water element.

Read and study about the following figures, and you will open your perceptions. You will also make yourself more receptive to the more ethereal realms of life.

- Aphrodite (Greek)—love and beauty goddess created when the sky impregnated the great sea womb

- Danaides (Greek)—daughters of Danaus condemned in Hades to pour water eternally into a bottomless vessel

- Naiads (Greek)—nymphs of brooks, springs and fountains

- Oceanus (Greek)—god of the outer sea encircling the Earth

- Poseidon/Neptune (Greco-Roman)—god of the sea

- Tiamat (Babylonian)—dragon woman of bitter waters

- Ran (Scandinavian)—goddess of the sea and queen of the drowned

- Ix Chel (Mayan)—snake goddess of water

- Aryong-Jong (Korean)—goddess who controlled rainfall

- Doda (Serbian)—goddess of rain

- Ningyo (Japanese)—fish goddess who, if eaten, would guarantee eternal youth and beauty

- Nimue (Celtic)—Lady of the Lake

- Ea (Babylonian)—god of the arts and the sea

Exercise #2:
Attuning to Water Spirits Through Faerie Tales

There are a variety of folk and faerie tales that provide insight into the character and personality of the spirits, sprites, nymphs and faeries associated with the element of water. These stories provide many clues as to how to approach and work with them. They also provide clues as to what you can expect from such contact. Be sure to keep in mind though that many of these tales are symbolic.

By reading what has been written about them in story, song and poetry, you send a message that you are open to contact. Just as with humans, if we show an interest in them, they will respond.

The list of tales that follows is by no means complete. It is a starting point for learning about the nature spirits and energies associated with the element of water. It will help you begin to change your perceptions and initiate your own relationship with this watery realm.

- *Sun, Moon and Water* (Nigerian)

- *Why Crab Has No Head and How the First River Was Made* (Nigerian)

- *The Discontented Fish* (Senegalese)

- *The Fountain of Speaking Waters* (United States)

- *How Coyote Brought Back People After the Flood* (Miwok)

- *The Crane and the Turtle* (Japanese)

- *The Tale of Deucalion* (Greek)

- *Jason and the Argonauts* (Greek)

- *Odysseus and the Sirens* (Greek)

- *Hercules and the Lernean Hydra* (Greek)

- *Gilgamesh, Upnapishtim and the Flood* (Sumerian)

- *The Tale of the Rainbow Snake* (Australian)

- *Lutey and the Mermaid* (British)

- *The Little Mermaid* (Danish)

- *The Mermen Laughed* (Icelandic)

- *The Seal's Skin* (Icelandic)

- *The Fisherman and His Wife* (German)

- *Water of Life* (German)

- *The Singing Drum and the Mysterious Pumpkin* (Bantu)

- *The Tale of Huldbrand* (German)

One of the most dynamic ways of opening to the nature spirits of the waters is by using the tales as a form of meditation. This is done in the same way as was described in the last chapter with those tales for the element of earth. Through this form of meditation, the tales becomes a bridge between your mortal world and the water realm of faeries.

1. This exercise is most effective when performed outside around a natural water source—a pond, a spring, a well, a rain pool, a river, etc. A place where you can place your feet in the water is very powerful for opening to the touch of the water spirits.

2. Find a time when you will be undisturbed. Choose a story that you are drawn to with water sprites, nymphs, mermaids or other water spirits. Re-read the story to familiarize yourself with it.

3. Now close your eyes and relax. Feel yourself connected to water. If you have not done it, place your feet in the water source. If nothing else, have a pool or bowl of rainwater that you can splash lightly over your face. Know that as you do this, you are activating your own watery elements, and you are calling forth your personal undine to help you attune to this element even more strongly.

4. Perform a deep breathing and progressive relaxation. You may even wish to buy a sound effects tape that has ocean sounds and rhythms to it.

5. As you relax with your eyes closed, visualize within your mind that you are sitting by the seashore. The waves roll in and break on the rocks and the beach around you. The sound is comforting in its continuousness. Occasionally, you can feel the spray lightly upon your face. The water has a hint of salt, and it makes you realize that here water and earth intersect.

   There is a soft mist, and the sea about you is a rich green, fertile with unseen life. The sun is barely visible against the horizon, and you are not sure if it is rising or setting. The air is fresh and clean and wisps of sea mist and fog are forming along the beach. They swirl and dance, as if actually coming to life out of the sea itself.

   This mist draws closer to you as you sit upon the rocks watching and listening to the rhythm of the waves. It tickles gently as it encircles you. It is comforting. It actually has a life of its own and all it seems to want to do is encircle and caress you with its nebulous touch. You feel safe and exhilarated, more alive than you have felt in ages, as it draws up around you.

Soon you are encloaked in this ethereal mist. The sea is lost to your vision and the sound of the waves grows fainter. Then the caressing mist begins to fade. As it does, you find that you are no longer sitting upon the rock by the shore.

6. At this point you visualize yourself as the main character in the faerie tale you have chosen. See yourself stepping into the story line. Imagine yourself interacting with the people, the faeries and other beings within the story.

7. You do not have to hold strictly to the story line. Adjust it according to your own will. Use your creative imagination. Remember that the imagination is part of the feminine energies and part of what those spirits of the watery element can help us awaken and use.

8. At the end of the story, visualize the sea mist rising up and surrounding you again. As it does, the sound of the waves begins to be heard once more. As the sea mist shifts and dances and moves over you and dissipates, visualize yourself sitting back on that rock overlooking the sea. Know that this shore is a borderland where the mortal world and the watery realm of faeries intersect. Know that each time you encounter such an intersection, even if only in a meditation, you will strengthen your connection to the water spirits.

9. Take slow, deep breaths and allow the scene to fade around you. The rocks disappear and so does the great sea. You feel yourself sitting on that spot in nature where you began your meditation. Still keeping your eyes closed, feel the water element. If your feet are immersed, wiggle them. Does the water feel different? Do you notice anything out of the ordinary.

10. Now slowly open your eyes and gaze softly into and around the water. Are there any shadows? Any glowing spots

within the water? Are there any shore creatures visible—frogs, turtles, dragonflies, lizards, etc.? Can you see any faces or scenes on the surface of the water? Do you feel as if you are being watched? Do you feel any touches or tingles upon the body? Pay attention to everything you feel.

Don't worry that you may be imagining it all. Remember that imagination does not mean the same thing as unreal. Give thanks to the element of water and those beings of it for sharing with you. And then go about your day's business, knowing that each time hereafter the connections and responses will grow even more tangible.

Exercise #3:
Meeting the King of the Undines

1. Begin this meditation just as you did the previous exercise. Find a time and place outdoors, if possible, where you will not be disturbed. A place where you can plant your feet in the water is most effective.

2. Now close your eyes and relax. Feel yourself connected to the water. You may even wish to splash your face lightly. Know that as you do this you are activating your own watery elements.

3. As you relax, with your eyes closed, visualize yourself sitting by the seashore. The sound of the waves is comforting in its continuousness. The rock upon which you sit occasionally catches a wave as it rolls in, and you feel its spray upon your face. It is stimulating, and the water has a hint of salt. It makes you realize that here water and earth intersect.

   The sea before you is a soft, rich green—fertile with unseen life. The sun is not visible against the distant horizon, and you are not sure if it is dawn or dusk. The sea air is soft, and as you look out at the expanse of water, you begin to see wisps of mist and fog.

   At first they are scattered, but they begin to grow and draw together. They swirl and dance, as if actually coming to life out of the sea itself. It begins to form along the beach so you cannot see where the shore ends and the water begins.

Within the shifting sea mist, you begin to make out a vague form. The mist actually seems to dance around it, as if it is the center of its life and activity. Somehow you know that this must be Nixsa, the king of the element of water. You whisper his name, more to yourself than to the waters, but the sea mist responds, shifting and dancing around the figure. It becomes more clearly defined.

A second time you speak the name, this time a little louder. It is done as if to test whether the mists will shift and dance in response again. The mist swirls and arches around the figure, and you begin to see it move.

Yet a third time you speak the name of Nixsa, sending it out strong and clear. The sea mist parts and Nixsa steps out from the water and onto the shore before you. His face is a soft shade of green, and his robe is a deeper, rich green, edged with the very foams of the ocean itself. His face shifts and changes, almost as if in response to each wave of the ocean itself. Throughout it though, his eyes hold your attention with great feeling.

He motions for you to follow him, and you stand and walk beside him along the shore. Before long you come to a rocky area which contains several tidal pools. He motions for you to sit beside one, and he steps into the middle of it. He bends and cups some of the water into his hands and holds it before you.

"This is the life blood of the Earth. Without it no life could be sustained here. Without it you could not exist. At its most primal level, your own blood is no different than this in my hands. All fluids are linked together, and one source of life fluid affects the others."

Nixsa turns his hands over and restores the water he cupped within them to the tidal pool below. He waves his hand across the surface of the pool, and scenes begin to appear. You see the life essence and energy of water everywhere. You see rivers, streams and ponds from all over the world, and then you see the Earth as if looking at it from a distant star with the blue waters covering most of its surface.

Again he passes his hand over the pool, and the images change. You see rivers and other natural water sources polluted with chemicals and toxic wastes, and you see beings both strange and disfigured by such activities. You see the life of the seas dying, and you see the vitality of crops and foods weakened by poor water. Then you see an image of the human body superimposed over the waters of the natural world. As these waters change, the human body responds.

As you observe, the body ages before your eyes. You are even able to see the flow of blood through the veins and arteries and to all of the organs of the body. In the beginning the blood is a glowing, vibrant shade of red—strong and healthy. As the body ages and is exposed to impure water sources and foodstuffs grown with them, the blood changes from a vibrant to a duller shade. The natural waters of the world have repercussions on the human body. It makes you feel tired, unclean and thirsty for pure waters.

"As a stream is polluted in the world, so the stream within your own body is polluted. As the waters are respected and harvested, your own life becomes respected and brings great harvest. Though humans try to believe otherwise, no part of the world is separate from them. Everything influences everything else."

Yet again, he passes his hand over the tidal pool. Now you see images of the water sources of the world that you had never expected. You see forms—faint and delicate—dancing upon the crests of waves. You see deep ocean creatures of life and vibrancy. You are shown beautiful devas and nymphs that surround and inhabit every natural source of water. You see creatures of the waters and shores that bring health and new compassion to the world. You see yourself—strong and vital—working, playing and living with them. You see a joint effort of both realms working together, and you see waters everywhere flowing strong and clean and pure.

"From the water comes great life, abundance and health. As you open to the watery world, you will have opportunity to work with those of this realm—to change what has gone before. You will learn to bring forth from the waters of your own life environment new inspiration and abundance."

Nixsa reaches again into the tidal pool, and he retrieves a beautiful coral-colored shell. He then fills it with water from the pool and pours part of it over your head. It is cool, and as it streams down your face, there is a slight stinging of the eyes, but it passes quickly.

You wipe your eyes and look again at Nixsa. He stands brighter and stronger before you. You see and feel his energy deep within your soul more intensely than ever before. The water has cleansed your vision.

The world around you has changed. Everything is clearer and cleaner. In the distance, bobbing upon the ocean's surface, are several beautiful mermaids, their eyes fixed lovingly upon you. Several dolphins jump from the depths a short distance from the shore, and you are positive that there are faeries riding upon them. Tiny water sprites are seen riding the crest of each wave, emitting soft musical laughter, as the waves break on the shore.

Nixsa holds the shell, still containing water, to your mouth and you drink. It is sweet and crisp. You never knew that water could taste like this. It fills you with a love for the waters and those beings of it. It also leaves you with a sense of longing for even more. Nixsa then places the shell in your hand.

"This is a sign of my promise to work with you and help open the mysteries of water to you. Do not be fooled by it though, for it carries great responsibility. Water is an intoxicating elixir, and if you accept this, you are promising to immerse yourself in it and fill your life with it. By accepting this shell, you accept the responsibilities and the joys of working with my kingdom and those within it for the betterment of all.

"If you are unsure of this commitment, leave the shell within this tidal pool. Here it will remain for you until such time as you choose to take it upon yourself. The choice is always yours."

Nixsa passes his hand over the tidal pool again, and the sea mist rises from it. As it surrounds and envelops him, he is drawn down into it, and as the mist dissipates, there is no sign of him. You stand, holding the shell in your hand.

You look out to the ocean, and there standing upon the crest of a wave you see the figure of Nixsa. Surrounding him are sprites and beings of the water element. A whale passes closely behind him, covering him in a shower of water. Then there is nothing but the ocean.

You look back to the tidal pool at your feet. You think about the water element and all that Nixsa told you. You look at the simple beauty of the shell in your hand and all of its significance. And you make your decision. As you do, the image of the ocean and the shore begins to fade, and you find yourself back where you started at the beginning of your meditation.

∾❋ⸯ

Excerpt From My Personal Journal

I began my chapter on water spirits early this morning. The owners of the apartment building were up early as well, preparing to continue their gutting of the open area. As I began my work on the water sprites, I noticed the weather changing. Although it started sunny, it grew increasingly cloudy.

As I finished the section on using rainwater and pools as a window to the faerie realm, the first raindrops began to fall. I couldn't help but smile. This was either one of the greatest coincidences or there were other forces at work. I believe the latter.

The rain began to pour down accompanied by tremendous thunder, and the work at the apartments was halted for the day. I decided to stop my work on the water sprites chapter as well. Somehow I knew if I continued, the next day the rain would also continue.

I began the next day with my meditation to connect with the water spirits, and I picked up where I left off. It was still cloudy outside, and as I worked, the rain began again, as it had off and on all night. The work of clearing the wild nature area was stopped for yet another day. I completed this chapter, but was left wondering what the contact with the air spirits would bring about in this situation . . .

(continued at the end of Chapter Six)

✥

Chapter Six

The Breath
of the Air Spirits

Air is as essential to life as is water. It is an active, creative element. It is symbolic of thought, memory and even freedom. It is air which connects the Earth with the heavens, and thus it also symbolizes higher mind and inspiration. Air is the creative breath.

Inspiration comes from the Latin word "spiritu"—meaning "to breathe." When we are inspired, we are linked with the breath of the divine.

Through breath and air, we assimilate power. The coming and going of air in the breathing process reflects the involution and evolution of life. Proper breathing is essential to our health. Learning to breathe with definite thought and meditation is a means of calling all beautiful things into being.

Air makes possible the power of sound and music. Learning to speak with greater life force is part of what those beings of the air can help us to do. They assist us in understanding this element and in liberating our own expression of divine breath so that we can use it to succeed in life. This divine breath though must be nourished with the right thought and action. The true power of the word is awakened with the aid of the spirits of the air.

From the softest sigh to the strongest gale, beings of the element of air can be found. They work to maintain the atmosphere and the formation of clouds. They function wherever the mind is being employed—especially in the creative, educational and communication processes. They work closely with those beings we often call angels, assisting them in their tasks. Often sylphs, faeries and other air spirits serve as temporary guardians until such time we are ready for our true holy guardian angel.

Those beings of the air element help us in understanding the working power of the mind. They assist us in empowering and controlling thought. Through the proper development of this power and their assistance, we learn that we control much of our spiritual path.

These beings range in size from the tiniest of sylphs to the larger storm faeries that move the winds and bring changes in the weather. There are also great air spirits that work to maintain and protect the atmosphere. These vary in shape and size according to the environment. Those in the higher altitudes are more ethereal and wispy in appearance than those functioning in the lower altitudes.

The faeries and spirits of the air vary in appearance, too. In general, they appear more delicate than those of the other elements. They often take a Tinkerbell-like form in many cases. Those of the larger size may actually appear more angelic, while still others often take the form of dragons, birds or other flying creatures.

Unlike those of the faerie realm associated with other elements, those of the air have no physical life upon which to develop and bind themselves. They have much more freedom of movement and can be found anywhere.

Many of those of this realm function in areas of service to humans. They are always found where healing is to occur. They work to alleviate pain and suffering. They serve as guardians, and they work in areas that help humans grow. They love children best of all. They actually love being able to serve, especially when the service brings tenderness, respect and creative experience.

The traditional magician's and witch's familiar is often part of this kingdom. Familiars can be defined as spirits (often of the air) with a close working relationship with humans. Most people assume that a familiar is the dog, cat or pet of the magician or witch, but the truth is that the spirit can be invoked and made to work through any form—animate or inanimate. This could be an animal, a crystal ball or a mirror.

> *In the fairy tale* Snow White and the Seven Dwarfs *the wicked queen talks to her magic mirror and the mirror answers her. Although it is not explained in the fairy tale, the voice of the queen's mirror, its awareness and identity, belong to a familiar spirit which the queen has bound within the glass through the use of her occult arts.**

When teaching public school, I thoroughly enjoyed the times my classes read *The Tempest* by William Shakespeare. This is the tale of a man by the name of Prospero who had a familiar spirit named Ariel. The discussions surrounding Ariel were always lively. Intriguing and mystifying, this tale serves to draw spirits of the air into the environment. It is interesting to note that on the days I assigned this play there were always strong winds and/or rain storms.

Of course, many stories relate how these familiars were forced into a working relationship with humans, but there are ways of inviting the services of an air spirit through love and respect. This in turn begets loyal affection and service. This takes time and patience, especially if we want the relationship to be one of benefit, pleasure and constancy.

We will not be exploring the process for invoking a familiar spirit within this work, but it is important to note that such spirits are most often those of the air realm. For more information, you may wish to consult Donald Tyson's *How to Make and Use A Magic Mirror* (Llewellyn Publications).

There are qualities that are universally attributed to most air spirits and faeries.

1. They are often very delicate and ethereal in appearance. They have great beauty and gentleness.

2. They communicate with us mostly through thought. They are critical to the development of clairaudience.

---

* Donald Tyson, *How to Make and Use a Magic Mirror*. (St. Paul, MN: Llewellyn Publications, 1990), p. 127.

3. They can help us in developing telepathy.

4. They have stimulating, changeable energy. It may be calm and refreshing or it may become gale-like in intensity. The ability to handle it is most determined by the the ability to control one's own mind.

5. Just as the wind takes many forms so do these faeries. They often take the form of birds or other winged creatures. Many bird spirit totems are spirits of the air using the bird form to connect with the human more directly. They will often appear in the form of butterflies as well. They can even take human form.

   There are a number of stories about faeries who use the form of birds. The Chinese tale of *The Crane Maidens* and the Norwegian tale of *The Swan Maiden* are but two examples. Occasionally such figures fly to shore and as they remove their cloak of feathers, they come forth as their true selves, beautiful spirit maidens. In most of these tales, by capturing one of the feathered cloaks, the maiden was bound to human form until the cloak was recovered.

6. Song and music draws them, especially music of wind instruments. They can add great power to our words and enhance the effects. Since air is essential to voice, this is only natural.

   Even something as simple as whistling can draw the air faeries to you.

   Choose a day on which the air is perfectly still. Go outside and sit under a tree. If you have access to one, take with you a flute or penny whistle. If you don't, simply sit under a tree and whistle softly a childhood tune that you enjoyed. By the second or third round, the air spirits and faeries arrive. The tree leaves will rustle. You may see some leaves or dust upon the ground swirl. A bird may land in the tree. A butterfly may appear. You will notice their arrival with a tangible sign.

7. They often reveal their presence through sudden breezes, fragrances or the finding of feathers.

8. They are generally not confined to any particular area.

9. They can stimulate great healing and wisdom. They can also stimulate musical abilities and inspiration.

10. They are essential to understanding all languages, including the languages of animals.

The faeries and spirits of the air are essential to spiritual initiation by air. This is the understanding of the workings and powers of the mind. Air separates Earth and heaven, and thus it is a link between our spirituality and our physical consciousness. The air faeries can facilitate the forging of this link.

They help us in opening to new wisdom—wisdom based on higher intuition. They assist us in transmuting psychic sensitivity into a spiritual sensitivity. The spirits and faeries of the air assist us in controlling our surroundings. Learning to control what we allow into our life is part of the lesson of the initiation of air, and part of what we learn to do by working with those beings of this element. They help us to recognize and use only that air that will strengthen and nurture us. They are here to help teach us that on the path to higher initiation, mental aspects are as important to us as physical life experiences. They teach us that whatever manifests in the physical is a result of the mind. They teach us that all energy follows thought.

The keynote of those faeries and beings of the air is strength and self-mastery. They help us with the lessons of discovering strength through overcoming obstacles. This is the lesson of harmony (found in music, which is the realm they rule). It takes great mental strength to overcome struggles and sorrows for greater creative expression within our life.

The mind in motion—air in motion—is a force. It is the wind. The wind can be used for either positive or negative purposes, for our benefit or our detriment. By learning to attune and work with these beings, we open access to both the energies of Earth and of heaven.

Many of the faeries of the air element are actually part air and part water. Often this kind is most evidently living in the clouds. Watching and meditating upon the clouds will reveal their presence. You can actually call on the faeries of the clouds and then think the clouds into specific shapes. This is good practice for attuning to the air faeries, as they can read our thoughts.

As mentioned earlier, whistling is a way of calling up the wind—and thus the wind faeries. When the great ships sailed the oceans, whistling was not permitted. They believed that whistling would invoke storm winds.

Through the faeries of the air we learn to make our wishes reality. They empower our thoughts. As we will see in Chapter Eleven, many faerie godmothers and patrons are those of the element of air.

Through learning to connect with the faeries and spirits of the air, we gain many benefits.

1. They enhance the power of speech and music.

2. They help us use the power of thought so that we can call all beautiful things into being.

3. They teach us the harmony of all things and all people, and they help create a desire for greater harmony.

4. They can help us develop telepathy and clairaudience.

5. They stimulate intuitiveness and inventiveness.

6. They are always drawn to those who write (and read) poetry, for poetry is the music of words.

7. They awaken greater intellect and strength of will.

8. They are essential in connecting with our genius.

    In the Greek tradition, there was a belief that each individual was assigned a daemon at birth. The daemon was a spirit that could guide and protect the individual throughout his or her life. In many ways it is like the traditional guardian angel, but it can also be likened to the genius aspect inherent to each individual's soul. The air spirits can help us learn to connect and draw upon its resources.

9. They help us in developing a more mystical attitude toward life.

10. They assist us in recognizing and using the winds of change in every aspect of our life—from determining the weather to everything that can occur within our lives.

Exercise #1:
Understanding the Air Element Through Myths

Just as with the other elements, there have been a variety of mythic figures and beings associated with the air element and the various forces it manifests. Many of these mythic figures demonstrate characteristics and behaviors similar to the air faeries and spirits. An examination of them will provide clues to understanding the forces we open to through connection with the air element.

Read and study about the following figures, and you will expand your perceptions of the faerie realm operating through the element of air. It will also make you more receptive to all of the more ethereal realms of life in general.

- Zeus (Greek)—god of the heavens

- Hera/Juno (Greco-Roman)—queen of the sky

- Boreas (Greek)—god personifying the north wind

- Iris (Greek)—winged rainbow goddess who traveled with the speed of the wind

- Lilith (Semetic)—winged lady of the air

- Odin (Nordic)—creator of the cosmos

- Frigg (Nordic)—goddess of the heavens

- Brahma (Hindu)—creator of heaven and earth sometimes depicted riding on a swan or a peacock

- Nut (Egyptian)—great sky goddess

- Anu (Assyro-Babylonian)—god of the sky

- Quetzalcoatl (Nahuatl)—god of the wind generally represented as a plumed serpent

- Indra/Svargapati (Indian)—lord of heaven

- Feng-Po (Chinese)—earl of the wind

- Feng-P'o-P'o (Chinese)—goddess of the wind who could be seen riding on a tiger among the clouds

Exercise #2:
Attuning to Air Spirits Through Faerie Tales

Many folk and faerie tales provide insight into sylphs, faeries and other air spirits. These stories can help draw them to you and provide clues on how best to work with them. Keep in mind that many of these stories are symbolic.

By reading what has been written about the spirits of the air in story, song and poetry, you invite their presence. Just as with all life forms, if you show an interest in them, they will respond, so remember to be patient and persistent.

The following list gives you a starting point for learning about the nature spirits and energies associated with the element of air. The stories will open your perceptions and help initiate your own personal relationship with the airy realm.

- *Raven Brings the Light* (Inuit)

- *The Thunder God* (Chinese)

- *The Tale of Father Frost* (Russian)

- *The Fall of the Sky* (Greek)

- *Daedalus and Icarus* (Greek)

- *The Seven Ravens* (German)

- *The Three Feathers* (German)

- *The Old Woman in the Forest* (German)

- *The Six Swans* (German)

- *The Three Languages* (German)

- *The Goose Girl* (German)

- *The Swan Maiden* (Norwegian)

- *The Crane Maidens* (Chinese)

- *The Fall of the Sky Maiden* (Iroquois)

- *The Wonderful Healing Leaves* (Jewish)

- *East of Sun, West of Moon* (Scandinavian)

- *The Flying Carpet, the Tube and the Apple* (Indian)

- *The Story of Perseus* (Greek)

- *The Tale of the Blue Hag* (Gaelic)

- *The Three Wishes* (French)

- *The Tempest* (British)

　　As we have seen with the other two elements, we can use these tales in a form of meditation to open to those of the faerie realm. Through this form of meditation, the tale becomes a bridge between the mortal world and the airy realm of faeries.

1. This exercise is most effective when performed outside, in an open field or on top of a hill. A day in which there are clouds and a nice breeze is even more effective. You want to be where you can feel the wind.

2. Find a time when you will be undisturbed. Choose a story that deals with the element of air or those faeries and beings that have an airy quality about them. Re-read the story to familiarize yourself with it.

3. Allow yourself to relax. Perform a progressive relaxation. You may wish to play a piece of flute music or a sound effects record that emulates wind. Anything that will help you attune to this element can be used.

4. Now close your eyes. Feel the air about you. If there is a breeze, notice the direction it comes from. How does it feel upon your face? Is it warm? Cold? Gentle? Can you hear it? If there are trees nearby, what sound does it make as it blows through them? Imagine that it is speaking to you as it does. Now breathe deeply of the air, and know that as you do you are calling forth your own personal sylph to help you attune to the element of air even more strongly.

5. As you relax, begin to visualize the scene changing around you. See yourself coming to the top of a rocky cliff. The air is strong and the sky is blue. The clouds look so close you feel as if you could almost touch them.

   You climb over the last few rocks and find yourself on the cliff's edge. From this perspective, you can see the whole world about you. The air is crisp and sweet, and you breathe deeply, feeling yourself energized and vitalized by it.

   The feel of the wind at this height is exhilarating, and you feel as if you could grow wings and fly. You raise your arms as if they were wings and you close your eyes, imagining what it would be like to be an eagle about to soar from this cliff.

   As you open your eyes, you see the clouds shifting and dancing before you. They seem to draw closer. They are so thick and white and soft. They begin to form around you, slowly encloaking you in their softness. Soon you cannot even see the cliff upon which you are standing.

The horizon is lost to your sight. The sky above is no longer visible. You are in a sea of clouds that shift and dance with each subtle breeze. Then the clouds begin to grow thinner. It is as if the wind is dissipating and scattering them about. And as they disappear, you find you are no longer upon that cliff, but in an entirely different scene.

6. At this point you visualize the primary scene of the faerie tale you have chosen for your meditation. See yourself as the main character, stepping into the story line. Imagine yourself interacting with the people, the faeries and the circumstances within that tale.

7. You do not have to hold strictly to the story line. Adjust it according to your own will. Use your creative imagination. Be inventive.

8. At the end of the story, visualize yourself being surrounded by cloud formations. As they form around you, you begin to hear the wind. The faerie tale scene is hidden from your view by the clouds.

Then the clouds begin to dissipate. You begin to see the open blue sky. At first you only feel the cliff beneath your feet, but as the last of the clouds dissipate, you see yourself standing strong and solid upon its edge.

The wind is strong and vitalizing, and as you look out over the expanse below, you are sure you can see forms moving in the wind. You begin to understand. This cliff is a borderland, a point where the mortal world and the airy realm of faeries intersect. You understand that each time you encounter and use this intersection, even if only in meditation, you will strengthen your connection to the air faeries.

9. Take slow, deep breaths. You feel the winds softening around you, and the scene begins to fade. The horizon disappears and so does the cliff upon which you are standing. You feel yourself sitting on that spot in nature where you first be-

gan this meditation. Keeping your eyes closed, again feel the air around you. Is there a difference? Does it feel warmer? Cooler? Softer? Can you hear it more clearly? What do you hear around you?

10. Now slowly open your eyes and gaze about you. Do you see any movements in the upper branches of trees? Are leaves rustling in response to you? What do you imagine they are saying? Are there any birds or butterflies or other winged creatures around you? Do you feel any touches or tingles on any part of the body? Pay attention to everything you see, feel and hear.

     Don't worry that you may be imagining it all. Remember that the imagination is not the same thing as unreality. Take a moment and give thanks to the element of air and those beings in it for sharing with you. Give thanks and acknowledgment to your own sylph. Breathe deeply of the air and notice how it makes you feel now. And then go about your day's business, knowing that each time hereafter the connections and responses will grow even more dynamic.

Exercise #3:
Meeting the King of the Sylphs

1. Begin this meditation just as you did the previous exercise. Find a time and place outdoors, preferably on a breezy day and where you will not be disturbed.

2. Now close your eyes and take several deep breaths to relax. You may even wish to perform a progressive relaxation at this point. With each breath, know that this act is possible only because of the sylphs. With your eyes closed, feel the air—the atmosphere around you. Notice how the breeze touches your face. If there is a breeze, listen closely. Can you hear it through the trees? Imagine that it is speaking to you. Now breathe deeply of the air once more, and know that as you do you are calling forth your own personal sylph to help you in meeting the king of the sylphs.

3. As you relax, begin to visualize the scene changing around you. See yourself climbing to the top of a rocky cliff. The air is stronger here. The sky looks so close and so blue. Even the clouds seem close enough to touch.

You climb over the last few boulders, and you find yourself on the cliff's edge. From this perspective, you can see the whole world about you. The air is crisp and sweet, and you breathe deeply, feeling yourself energized and vitalized by it. You feel as if you are truly awakening—as if from a deep sleep.

The feel of the wind as it gusts and blows at this height is exhilarating. It makes you feel as if you could grow wings and soar. You even raise your arms slowly as if they were wings and you close your eyes. You imagine for a moment that you are an eagle about to soar from this cliff. You can even feel the wind ruffling your feathers. It is enticing and powerful, and you know you must be careful or the power of air may actually draw you off the cliff.

You open your eyes, and you see the clouds shifting and dancing before your eyes. They seem to be drawing closer. They are so thick and soft, you feel as if you could easily step from the cliff and be supported by them.

They begin to gather before you, like the clouds you have seen gather before storms. Within the shifting clouds, you begin to make out a vague form. The clouds actually seem to be moving around it, as if it is the center of their life and activity. Somehow you know that this must be Paralda, king of the element of air.

You whisper his name—more to yourself than to the clouds—but the clouds respond. You feel a soft gust of air blow over you, and the clouds shift even more. The figure in the center becomes more clearly defined.

A second time you speak the name—this time a little louder and bolder. You feel a stronger gust of air and the clouds shift and dance in response. They draw back a bit, and you see the figure become more distinct and even begin to move.

Yet a third time you speak the name of Paralda. You sing it out loud and clear, knowing that the air may carry it for miles from this height. The clouds part, and Paralda steps from their midst and onto the cliff's edge to stand before you. He is tall and slender with an elf-like face. The eyes are silver, but they shift like clouds moving across the heavens. His hair is long and silvery and flows around him as if he is constantly standing in the midst of wind. He is dressed in a white robe, lined in blue. It billows about him—dancing constantly with every movement of air no matter how soft.

He moves to stand beside you on the cliff, looking out at the expanse of sky. He raises his hand and a cloud forms within it, and he draws it down and holds it before you. As you reach to touch it, a soft breeze blows over you and the cloud dissipates into nothing. Paralda laughs softly at your surprise, and the winds blow in response to his laughter.

"Without air, there is no life. You could not exist—nor anything else upon the planet. Wherever there is space upon the planet, there is air, for we do not live in a vacuum. This humans have yet to learn. We breathe air. We move through air. And we use air every time we speak or think."

His voice is expressive and changes, and with it the air about you changes. His speaking fills the atmosphere around you with great winds one moment and soft breezes the next.

"We are all affected by what air—what atmosphere—we are exposed to. We leave traces of our being within the air—every where we go. The words we speak, the thoughts we think and the attitudes we assume affect the atmosphere. Even if only breathing, you have an effect or are affected."

Paralda motions for you to gaze out over the edge of the cliff. As you do, clouds begin to gather again, and they begin to shape themselves. Images begin to form in their midst. You see the atmosphere surrounding the Earth and the movement of air currents.

Then the images change, you see places in your life that made you uncomfortable. You see the air in those environments thick and discolored and erratic. You see scenes where individuals spoke negatively to you, and you watch as the air around you darkens and thickens. You see yourself carrying that discolored air with you from those places. You see those times in which you have thought or spoken ill of others, and you see those words and thoughts carried on invisible currents to infect the atmosphere around the individual. You never knew words and thoughts could carry so strongly.

You see those times you made others feel better by something you said. You see those times in which you have thought positively of individuals and situations, and you observe all of the effects upon them. You see places upon the Earth in which positive thoughts, prayers and rituals were performed, and you watch as others who visit these spots—not knowing their history—leave with new hope. You see the times and places and people in your life who made you feel better about who you are. And you see the atmosphere—the air—surrounding them and yourself from such occasions. And you begin to understand.

"For most people, these currents are temporary, and they dissipate quickly, but the more we harbor certain thoughts or speak the same words, the greater and more powerful the effect becomes. As people live and breathe those thoughts and words, the more it begins to affect them in the physical—for good or bad."

Again the clouds shift and different scenes begin to appear. You see places on the Earth that are thick with smog and fumes. You see beings in those areas, disfigured by such pollution. You see life and vitality being choked, as the atmosphere becomes choked. You see breakdowns in communication occurring around the world as a result.

"By learning to attune to the element of air and those of us who work through it, you can become more sensitive to all the atmospheres you enter. You can recognize which environments you will want to avoid, which people may cause problems and which ones may be of most benefit. You will learn to change environments through a word, sound, thought or breath."

Yet again images form in the clouds before you. You see yourself sending thoughts with vibrancy and color to heal and bless others near and far. You see beautiful beings of the air that bring fresh inspiration and vitality. You see yourself working with them, and as you do you see broken communications mended. You see all atmospheres fresh and crisp and clean.

Paralda extends his hand out over the cliff and it disappears into the clouds before you. As he withdraws it, you see that he is holding a beautiful silver feather. He places it behind your ear. The winds begin to swirl and dance and the beings of the air draw closer. You hear them singing in the breezes and it fills you with joy. The sky is filled with birds soaring upon the winds and singing out to you, and you understand them.

"This is a sign of my promise to work with you and help open the mysteries of air to you. Air is powerful, and many societies worshipped air as the source of all life. It is exhilarating and it can manifest many things. By learning to work with it, you learn the true creative power behind thought and word.

"This carries great responsibilities. For if you accept this, your words and your thoughts will grow in strength with each passing second. Every breeze will give you greater power. That which you affectionately speak and think will be felt more lovingly. Cutting thoughts and words will wound more deeply.

"If you are unsure of this commitment, leave the feather upon this cliff. Here it will remain until such time as you choose to take it upon yourself. The choice is always yours."

The winds on the cliff begin to pick up. Paralda steps from the cliff's edge and hovers in the air before you. He nods, and the clouds encloak him. Then a gust blows across the clouds, moving toward the distant horizon, and the clouds dissipate. The only sign of Paralda is the sound of the wind.

You take the feather from behind your ear. You look out over the horizon, and you watch the birds soar. You look at the simple beauty of the feather and you are amazed that such a creation can enable them to fly. So simple and yet so powerful. You make your decision. As you do, the image of the cliff and the sky begins to fade. You find yourself back where you started at the beginning of your meditation.

～✤～

Excerpt From My Personal Journal

As I prepared to begin my work on the chapter on air spirits, I used the meditation from this chapter to attune to the air spirits to find what was about to occur next. Halfway through my meditation, a cool breeze began to blow through my room, again confirming the effectiveness of this meditation.

Upon completion, I looked outside and saw the rain clouds of the past two days breaking up. With the breeze picking up, the mugginess that had increased with the rain began to lesson. The rains had been good, but they were not cooling. Then I remembered that the sylphs control much of the weather and its changes. I am still amazed how easy it is to call them forth and feel their presence.

As the day moved on, the breeze remained and the temperatures dropped, and a long awaited cool spell brought forth relief from the heat. Unfortunately, it also brought forth renewed work on gutting the land behind my house . . .

(continued at the end of Chapter Seven)

᷂

Chapter Seven

The Warmth
of the Fire Spirits

Fire first belonged to the gods. In many societies are ancient myths of fire-stealers. One of the most well-known examples is the Greek tale of Prometheus who stole fire from Zeus so that humans could live. For this sacrifice, he was chained to a rock while an eagle tore at his liver.

Fire has always been regarded as something mysterious. The manner in which smoke melts into the air was considered magical. Even today, we give a great deal of significance to the power of fire. This is reflected in the way it is still used within our everyday speech. We have wildfires, forest fires, a sea of flames and bonfires. We have fireworks and fiery tongues. We fire salutes, and we get fired up about things. We even have fire-eaters. And expressions such as "light my fire," "carrying a torch" and "flames of passion" further demonstrate how fire has permeated all aspects of our life in one way or another.

The beings of the fire realm also permeate all aspects of our life. They are much more varied than what we often imagine. There are, of course, the tiny salamanders who are found wherever there is flame or heat. The flames of candles and fireplaces can be wonderful places to introduce yourself to fire faeries. Simply allow yourself to relax and focus on the flame(s). Watch as it dances and moves. As you gaze at the fire, allow your mind to follow the flames. You will begin to notice tiny forms within the flames themselves. You will begin to notice faces appearing and disappearing.

There are also smoke spirits and sun faeries, riding each ray of light. There are fire spirits within the molten centers of the Earth and living in volcanic areas. There are fire spirits who manifest through lightning.

There are fire faeries that work closely with and assist our own personal salamander. This includes those who align with us for the activation and control of the kundalini energy. The kundalini is an Eastern Sanskrit term meaning "coiled." It is the serpent energy. It represents the primal creative energy that unites and activates our energy centers. It is linked to primal sexual energy, but it is the seat of energy used for all creative activity. It is the creative life fire that opens us to new consciousness.

There are fire faeries of sexuality, drawn to wherever the sexual act is occurring. They serve to heighten the fires of sexual response. Some of the fire faeries are drawn to and work specifically with those passionate about a creative activity—especially musical composers. While their energy is easily directed and controlled through the creative activity, it can be difficult to find appropriate channels for their energies outside of such activities.

Many of the great classical composers led very passionate, turbulent and often emotionally unstable lives. Mozart, Schumann and

Wagner are but a few. Although there is no actual proof, when we consider the influence of fire spirits upon the emotions, it is likely that their presence may have augmented such conditions. While the music was a controlling channel for the fire spirit influence during composition and performance, there was no such balanced channel for their influence in other avenues of their lives.

There are also those of the fire realm who sometimes—although rarely—serve as patrons or patronesses. This will be covered more in Chapter Eleven when we discuss faerie godmothers. Those who do serve in this category often appear in the traditional genie form, as is depicted in some of the myths and tales from Persia and the Middle East.

There are fire faeries and spirits who work with our personal mundane fires—stimulating body heat, eroticism and physical energy, etc. There are also fire faeries and spirits who assist us with our spiritual fires—developing mysticism, clarity of spiritual thought, etc. Wherever we perform rituals, fire spirits will be found, especially in those rituals performed to stimulate any form of fertility.

Those of the fire realm are the most difficult to work with. They are very aloof, as fire is both destructive and creative. Although some societies have worshipped fire gods and goddesses above all else, most societies have held its force in great awe.

The fire faeries and spirits are the most difficult to control many times. This is not just because the energy is so dynamically primal. There is that, but it is because they are so very intelligent—often so much more than the faeries and spirits of the other realms. Their intelligence has given them what seems to be a great sense of independence.

Another reason they are difficult to understand and attune to is that they are always moving. Except for those of specific environments (molten areas within the Earth, volcanoes, etc.), many of them move freely about. Wherever a flame is being ignited, they move to that area. Wherever heat is stimulated, they move to that area.

I have heard that of all the beings of the faerie realm, these seem to have the least interest and curiosity about humans. I have not found this to be true, although they are a bit more difficult to detect and to work with, and they can initially show great indifference.

They are always around where human fires and flames are being stimulated—physical or otherwise. They have such a vitalizing effect they can stimulate strong emotional currents and passions

that can be difficult to control. Most humans have difficulty handling exceedingly stirring emotions, but with patience and self-discipline, a working relationship with them can become more intimate, powerful and beneficial.

There are qualities that are universally attributed to most fire faeries and spirits.

1. They are called into being by the rhythms of fire and manifestation of heat.

2. They often appear in shades of colors associated with fire (i.e. reds, oranges and yellows; this includes those spirits working through smoke and lightning).

3. Although they do not take forms of animals and other creatures frequently, they will occasionally do so. They most commonly appear in the form of dragons and other mythical fire creatures (see Chapter Ten), fireflies, snakes and other reptiles.

4. Music and strong rhythms are very enticing to them.

5. They stimulate great passion (sexual and otherwise).

6. They often appear in more of a masculine form, but we must be careful about drawing assumptions based on the form and the frequency of that form.

7. Although more numerous in warmer climates and seasons, they are not confined to any particular area. During the summer, they accumulate solar energy that will sustain them through the cooler winter months.

8. They can be dynamic catalysts for change and transformation. They are agents for the processes of destruction and creation.

9. They hold the keys to the lessons of life after death and the mysteries surrounding it. This is most evidenced by the fire spirit that uses the form of the mythical phoenix which rises from its own ashes (refer to Chapter Ten).

10. They instill great inspiration and spiritual perception, and
they hold the keys to the magical processes of alchemy.

The fire faeries and spirits operate within all aspects of life and
not just within the physical aspects of fire itself. They operate in everything from body heat to solar fires, from the fires of intellect to the
fires of the soul's development. They are here to assist humanity
through the fire initiation.

Part of this initiation is the traditional baptism of fire. This en-
compasses the trials of strength. In this we begin to open our eyes so
that we can see the dross that must eventually be burned out. It also
involves discovering our true relationship with others and what
those relationships teach us about ourselves. The turmoils—the
changes—are the fires of our experience. Each person shows us
something about ourselves. We may not always like it, and we may
even try to ignore it, regardless, we should try to learn from it, as difficult as it can be. Knowledge, like fire, can burn.

Through the fire faeries and spirits, we learn to distinguish between fire and flame. Fire is the force that lies behind the physical
manifestations of all flames. Through them, we learn to utilize the
forces of fire—be they the forces found within the flames of candles
or the flames of inspiration.

Fire brings more than just warmth. It also brings light. It enables us to see. As we learn to connect with the fire faeries, we also learn how spiritual and physical fire is operating within our lives and our consciousness. Our perceptions extend, and we begin to see the infinite possibilities for new growth created by the fires of life's experiences.

Through learning to connect with the faeries and spirits of fire, we gain many benefits.

1. They enhance our passions—physical and spiritual.

2. They can become agents of transmutation, transformation and regeneration.

3. They stimulate greater understanding of the primal love of spirit and our own creative life force.

4. They assist us in awakening, developing and controlling kundalini energy.

5. They assist us in seeing that which needs to be torn down and that which can help us re-create in our lives.

6. They teach us the physical and spiritual aspects of alchemy.

7. They stimulate creativity, courage, higher vision and idealism.

8. They can help prevent us from dissipating our life force through self-indulgence and sensual excess.

9. They help us to bring forth our own spiritual fires so that matter becomes obedient to the will. The force of our spiritual fire is the primal force of creative expression.

10. They help us in recognizing the laws of cause and effect as they are manifesting within our own life or the lives of others. They can assist us in making the laws of cause and effect work for us in every avenue of life.

11. They assist us in developing great catalytic healing energies.

12. They can teach us the true significance, power and applications of sexual energy—physically and spiritually.

Exercise #1:
Fire Faeries and Fire Readings

One dynamic and simple way of learning to attune and work with fire faeries and spirits is through psychic fire readings. It enables you to work with their energies to extend your perceptions. (Remember that one quality of fire is light.)

Forms of fire divination and scrying have been employed in various societies. Pyromancy is the technical name for utilizing fire and smoke for divination purposes. This could be as simple as interpreting which way the flame moves in response to questions. It could also involve carving questions on wood or writing it on parchment and then setting it upon the fire. The resulting flames and smoke would provide the clues to the question's answer.

Fire divination used to be the domain of the shamans, priests and priestesses. It was often performed in a ritualistic manner and after strict preparations. It is becoming a scarce tradition, as there are few who are capable of utilizing it to its fullest extent. This is sad, for it is a powerful way of opening the psyche. Although some fire rituals still require strict preparations, the average person can easily learn to do his or her own variation of a fire reading with some basic knowledge.

Some people that perform fire readings only do so at certain times of the year, such as on New Year's Eve to foresee the upcoming year's patterns. Others use it every time they build a fire. Some use it to answer basic questions and achieve solutions to current problems. Others use it to detect spirit guides, determine life patterns, uncover past life information and foretell the future.

A fire reading is a means of opening your own psyche to the subtle energies, patterns and forces around you. It invites the fire faeries and spirits into your environment, with the express purpose of heightening your psychic perceptions. Through the fire, they can help you to determine and detect spirit guides, as well as patterns for the future. Each time you read fire, your ability to perceive and respond to the fire faeries and spirits will increase.

Fire stimulates contemplation. It draws you into it. It has a hypnotic effect. The rhythm of the flames, their movement, the crackling sound all work together to induce an altered state of consciousness. You are more relaxed and your perceptions are heightened.

Fires will also change according to what is fueling them. Different kinds of wood will burn at different temperatures and intensity of flame. An examination of the tree spirits in Chapter Nine and the qualities of those trees can give you ideas about choosing the wood appropriate to the intention of the reading. For example, apple wood is powerful to burn in fire readings for perceiving mythic beings and creatures that are in your life. Pine wood can facilitate readings of past lives. Birch bark and oak are effective for any sort of fire reading.

The form and activity of the flames alter according to the substance they are feeding upon. Our thoughts and what intent we put into the building of the fire will affect how the flames and fire spirits will respond.

There are a number of ways of performing fire readings. The method below is one of the simplest, and it will invite the fire faeries, salamanders and fire spirits more tangibly into your life.

1. Any fire is sufficient to do a fire reading. A small bonfire outside is very effective. A fire in the fireplace can be a dynamic tool for communing with the fire faeries. Even the fire of a single candle can be used although a larger fire is more effective for a reading. If you do use candles, I suggest using a number of them and forming them into a circle no greater than twelve inches in diameter in front of you. The circle will provide a sacred space in which the flames, smoke and heat can manifest images and other psychic phenomena for your perception.

2. I have found that a fire reading at night is much more effective than during the day. The reason I believe this is so is because the light of the fire, juxtaposed against the darkness of the night, creates an intersection between the worlds. It is thus much easier to connect with the fire faeries. Midnight is also an intersection, and it can enhance the effects even more. Whatever time you choose, do it deliberately.

3. Take time prior to the lighting of the fire to meditate and think about the essence of fire, its symbolism and all of the

beings associated with it. Take time to visualize your purpose for the reading. Make sure you visualize the fire responding to you and giving forth the information you seek.

4. Gather the material for your fire. On a piece of parchment or on a piece of wood, write out what it is you wish to have the fire reveal to you. When you perform the meditation and visualization discussed above, have this on you. Hold it against the heart, the internal center for fire. Perform a deep, rhythmic breathing. With each breath, know that this piece of parchment or wood is becoming charged with your intent. Know that this intent will help shape the flames and smoke of the fire itself so that it will reveal what you seek.

5. As you light the fire, do so with full intent. Don't think of it as starting a fire, but as *creating* fire. You are creating fire and light where there was none. You are sending out a call throughout the entire universe, inviting those of the fire realm to assist you. See the fire as the creation of a doorway between your world and the world of faeries. As this doorway lights up, know that your own aura will brighten and strengthen as a result of this communion.

6. Take a seated position in front of the fire. Choose a distance that is comfortable. (If possible, refrain from placing a screen in front of the fire throughout the reading.) Take a deep breath. Allow the heat and light to dance over you. Feel the fire. Know that as the flames rise, the activity and presence of the fire faeries and spirits grows stronger. Try and see the flames as actual living beings.

7. When you feel yourself becoming entranced and dazed by looking into the fire, take your piece of wood or parchment and set it in the midst of the fire itself. (If you are using candles, have a metal plate or bowl inside the inner circle of candles. Ignite the parchment from one of the candles, and set it in that metal plate to burn.)

8. Now pay attention to the smoke and the flames. Allow yourself to become lost in the fire itself. Just relax and watch. Use a soft focus, that kind of dazed, staring-into-nothingness

look we get when daydreaming. Simply observe and note what you see.

Do the flames seem to go more to the right or left? Is the smoke darker or thinner? Do you see any faces and forms? Is your mind wandering? (Don't worry about this. With fire readings, the mind wandering is often psychically related. Those scenes you wander to often reflect what is going to happen or has a likelihood of happening. These can be literal or symbolic.)

Pay attention to everything you see or imagine you see within the fire. It all has significance. Most people, even on their first attempt, usually at least see faces: spirit guides, friends and relatives who have passed on, individuals who are coming back into their life, individuals who will be very important in the days ahead, etc.

9. Think about each thing you wrote on the parchment or wood. Focus on it, and speak it silently or audibly to the fire itself. It will respond. Watch, imagine and trust.

10. Once you have gotten the answers, allow the fire to burn itself out. Give thanks to those fire faeries, salamanders and fire spirits for communicating to you through the fire. Send them a blessing.

Do not spend more than a half hour on this initially. Remember that fire beings have a powerful influence. They can be over-stimulating. We want to learn to work with them in a controlled manner. It is easy to become lost in the enchantment of fire.

Take time at the end to record what you have seen, thought you imagined or any other perceptions you may have had. You will find that by recording them, they will make themselves even clearer. Also you will have something to refer back to, to determine the effectiveness each time you use this method.

Pay close attention to your dreams after a fire reading. The fire spirits will often continue their communication in the dream state.

Experiment with this method. Remember that the fire faeries and spirits help stimulate creative expression. You will soon find yourself inspired to work with them in your own unique manner.

Exercise #2:
Fire Faeries and Smoke Billets

A billet is a tool for the development of clairvoyance and for manifestations of psychic phenomena. It is used today most often by spiritualists. An individual will write his or her name and birth date on a piece of paper—sometimes with specific questions. The individual then holds it for several minutes to further "charge" the paper with his or her energy. The paper is then given to the medium or psychic and through psychometry (touching the paper), clairvoyant information is relayed to the individual whose name is on the paper.

Psychometry is the faculty for divining facts and information about an object or a person to whom the object belongs. By signing one's name to the billet, the piece of paper, a physical link is established that helps the psychic to attune more readily to the individual.

A smoke billet operates a little differently, for it employs faeries of fire and smoke to imprint upon the billet images important to the individual. The billet is signed just as described above. Then the medium or psychic holds the paper above a lit candle. It is moved around so that smoke and fumes from the candle accumulate on the paper. The psychic then looks at the smoke pattern and tries to see images and patterns within it. Sometimes they reveal faces, events, symbols, etc. These are then interpreted for the individual whose name is upon the billet.

You do not have to be a psychic or a medium to be able to use smoke billets. It is, in fact, a wonderful way to attune to the fire faeries, work with them and at the same time develop your own higher intuition. The process is simple.

1. You will need a candle for this exercise. I recommend that any candle you use be used strictly for this. You may use the same candle over and over again, but don't use a candle for smoke billets that you also use for other purposes. A red or an orange candle, or of any color that symbolizes fire will enhance the effects. If unsure, simply use a white candle.

   Make sure you dress and bless the candle for your purpose. You may anoint the candle by rubbing various oils into it (from the center out towards each end). While you do this, concentrate on the purpose of this candle—to invoke fire spirits for stimulating clairvoyant information through smoke billets. Visualize the fire faeries gathering and fulfilling what you wish to accomplish. Saying a prayer with the candle, dedicating it to its purpose, is also beneficial. You may wish to include the names of the archangel and the king of the fire element in this prayer (Michael and Djinn).

For more information on preparations of candles, you may wish to consult *Practical Candleburning Rituals* by Raymond Buckland (Llewellyn Publications).

2. You will also need paper. You may use any size paper, but a six-inch by six-inch piece is efficient. Parchment is also more effective than regular paper, as the smoke runs more, forming more intricate patterns.

3. Choose a time in which you will not be disturbed. Now write your name and birth date on a piece of the paper you have prepared. Hold it in the heart/solar plexus area with both hands, and begin to perform rhythmic breathing. Inhale for a count of four, hold for a count of four and exhale for a count of four. As you do this, visualize this paper becoming charged with your essence and your purpose. After several minutes of this, allow your breathing to become slow and regular.

4. Close your eyes now and perform a progressive relaxation. Keep holding the paper against you while you do this. Take time to reflect upon the element of fire, its significance and the fire faeries and elementals that will be drawn to you through this exercise. Visualize them forming the smoke in patterns on the paper that will enable you to detect spirit guides, along with other significant symbols and information.

5. Now light the candle. Know that as you do, you are participating in a creative act. You are creating fire and light where there was none. As the candle flame comes to life, see it as a call going forth to the fire spirits to work with you. You may even offer up a "thank you" in appreciation for their help ahead of time.

6. Now take the billet and hold it several inches above the flame of the candle. You want it close enough that the heat and smoke will accumulate, but not close enough to burn it. With practice you will determine what works best. (It will vary according to the quality of the candle.)

7. Slowly move the paper around in different patterns and circles over the flame. Try and cover as much of the middle section of the billet as possible. It's okay to occasionally pull it away and check the coverage.

8. Now hold the smoke billet in front of you, and just let yourself relax as you gaze at the smoke patterns on it. What do you see? Do any of the patterns resemble anything? Don't worry that it might be your imagination. Those images you see will have significance for you or you would not have been able to discern them—imagined or not. The billet is a tool to activate your clairvoyance with the aid of fire faeries. Look for faces, symbols, objects and anything that you personally can see within the smoky pattern upon the paper. Turn the paper in various directions to make sure you see it from all perspectives.

9. Take your time with this. You will see images within the paper. It will be up to you to determine the significance of those images. Faces may be spirit guides, relatives who have passed on or even symbolic of certain activities you may encounter in the day ahead. Trust your instincts. Remember that fire faeries heighten perceptions and however you interpret the images will probably be correct. It is beneficial to record your perceptions and the date. If you can do this on the back of the billet, it can serve as a wonderful record.

10. Give thanks to the fire faeries for what they have helped bring you. Extinguish the candle and put it away until next time.

    Save the billet; do not discard it. It is sometimes beneficial to wrap the billet in plastic and place it where it can't be disturbed for several days. Go back and look at it again each of the next two days. The interesting thing about most smoke billets is that they will change over time. Images will become more distinct, or entirely new images may appear. You will see this happen even in this short period of time.

Hold on to the billet for several months, and occasionally go back and re-examine it. Do you detect anything new? Did what you detected the first time bear itself out for you in any way? You may even wish to keep a scrapbook of smoke billets. In many ways it is like a photo album, depicting your growing relationship with the fire faeries.

Exercise #3:
Understanding the Fire Element Through Myths

Just as with the other three elements, there are a variety of mythic figures and beings associated with the fire element and the various manifestations of its force. Many of these mythic figures demonstrate characteristics and behaviors similar to the fire faeries and spirits. An examination of the myths will provide clues to understanding the force of fire that we open to by connecting with the fire faeries and beings.

Read and study about the following figures, and you will expand your perceptions of the faerie realm operating through the element of fire. It will also enhance your receptiveness to all ethereal realms of life.

- Typhoeus (Greek/Sicilian)—monster whose shoulders bore a hundred dragons' heads, each with a darting black tongue and eyes which spurted searing flame

- Agni (Hindu)—god of fire and guardian of man

- Surya (Hindu)—dazzling sun god

- Ra (Egyptian)—sun god

- Arinna (Phoenician)—sun goddess

- Xiuhtecuhtli (Nahuatl)—god of fire

- Brigid (Celtic)—fire goddess

- Hestia (Greek)—goddess of the hearth

- Hephaestus/Vulcan (Greco-Roman)—god of fire and metal-working

- Mahui-Iki (Polynesian)—queen of the fiery underworld

- Apollo (Greek)—god of the sun

- Prometheus (Greek)—Titan who stole fire from Olympus and gave it to man

- Latiaran (Irish)—goddess who carried a "seed of fire"

- Loki (Scandinavian)—fire demon

- Farbauti (Scandinavian)—god who gave birth to fire

- Ushas (Hindu)—dawn goddess said to be either the mother or lover of the sun

- Maia/Feronia (Greco-Roman)—fire goddess who ruled the forces of growth and warmth, including sexual heat

- Tu-Njami (Siberian)—mother fire

Exercise #4:
Attuning to Fire Spirits Through Faerie Tales

Many folk and faerie tales provide insight into the fire spirits and beings. These stories can help draw them to you more tangibly, and they can provide clues on how best to work with them.

By reading what has been written about the spirits of fire, you invite their presence. Just as with all life forms, if you show an interest in them, they will respond, so be patient and persistent.

The following list is a starting point for learning about and working with the spirits of fire. The stories will expand you perceptions and help initiate a more personal relationship with them.

- *Aladdin and His Wonderful Lamp* (Chinese/Middle Eastern)

- *The Tinder Box* (Danish)

- *Beauty and the Beast* (European)

- *Loki and the Treasures of the Gods* (Nordic)

- *The Necklace of Brising* (Nordic)

- *Snake Magic* (Swahili)

- *The Fire Children* (West African)

- *The Fire on the Mountain* (Ethiopian)

- *St. George and the Dragon* (British)

- *St. Dunstan and the Devil* (British)

- *The Firefly Princess and Her Lovers* (Japanese)

- *Prometheus and the Stealing of Fire* (Greek)

- *Phaethon and Apollo's Chariot* (Greek)

- *Moses and the Burning Bush* (Biblical)

- *Daughter of the Sun* (Cherokee)

As with the other elements, we can use tales as a form of meditation to open to those fire spirits and faeries. Through this form of meditation, the tale becomes a bridge between the mortal world and the fiery realm of faeries.

1. This exercise is most effective when performed outside where you can sit or lie in the sun. Warm, sunny days with few or no clouds is most effective. You may also perform this with great effects by sitting in front of your fireplace or even by having a lit candle in front of you.

2. Find a time when you will be undisturbed. Choose a tale that reflects the element of fire or those faeries and beings that have a fiery quality about them. Re-read the story to familiarize yourself with it.

3. Allow yourself to relax. Perform a progressive relaxation.

4. If you haven't already, close your eyes. Feel the sun on your face and body (if you are performing this outside). If sitting before your fireplace, feel the heat. How does it feel? Imagine you are being caressed by the heat of the sun. Feel yourself drawing the warmth and light into your body. Breathe deeply of its energy, and know that as you do, you are calling forth your own personal salamander to help you attune to the element of fire even more strongly.

5. As you relax, begin to visualize the scene changing around you. You are standing at the base of a great volcano. The earth about you is charred and parched. Steam rises from cracks in the earth. The sun is strong upon your face. The whole area seems parched and lifeless.

   Although the sun is warm upon you, it is not uncomfortable. In fact, you find it stimulating and powerful. With each breath, you seem to draw more of its energy into you. As you take in your breath, the earth trembles slightly and flame and steam erupt suddenly from the mouth of the volcano above you. The colors are so bright and strong, the sun is lost behind them. And then just as suddenly, all is still.

   You are not afraid. Somehow you know, that in spite of the activity, there is no danger. You are thrilled at being able to observe such a powerful sight. And then again, you feel the earth tremble beneath your feet. Steam rises from the fissures at the base of the volcano. You look about you, amazed as the steam shifts and dances. It thickens and seems to move toward you from all directions.

   As it begins to form around you, encloaking you, you are amazed at its softness. It is warm and soothing, and it has a gentleness to it that is exciting.

   The volcano above you is lost to your sight. Even the sky is no longer visible as you are lost in the swirling steam. And then it begins to diminish. It shifts and dances, breaking up, scattering. As the steam dissipates and recedes, you find you are no longer standing at the base of the volcano, but you are now in an entirely different scene.

6. At this point, visualize the primary scene of the faerie tale you have chosen for your meditation. Visualize yourself as the main character, stepping into the story line. Imagine yourself interacting with the people, the faeries and the element of fire itself found within the circumstances of this tale.

7. You do not have to hold strictly to the story line. Adjust it according to your own will. Use your creative imagination.

8. At the end of the story, visualize yourself being surrounded again by steam rising up from the ground. As it forms around you, you faintly hear the deep rumbles of the volcano. The faerie tale scene is hidden completely from view by the steam.

   As the steam begins recede, you see the open sky and feel the warmth of the sun—strong and healing—upon your body. You feel the volcanic earth beneath your feet, and you see yourself again standing at the base of that great volcano.

   Tiny flames erupt from the mouth of the volcano and from some of the fissures in the earth. You are not afraid. At that moment you are sure that you see forms and faces within the flames and steam. You begin to understand. This volcano—and even each tiny fissure—is more than just an opening in the earth. This is a point where the mortal world and the faerie realm intersect. You understand that each time you encounter and use this intersection, even if only in meditation, you will strengthen your connection to the fire faeries, spirits and salamanders.

9. Take slow, deep breaths. As you do, the area begins to become hazy. Soon the entire scene fades. The volcano disappears, and so does the charred earth beneath you. You feel yourself sitting upon that spot in nature where you first began this meditation. Keeping your eyes closed, feel the warmth of the sun or the fire. Is there a difference in the way

it feels now? Does it make you feel anything in particular? Can you hear it speaking to you?

10. Now slowly open your eyes and gaze about. As you look about, watch the sunlight reflect off of the trees and grass. Do you catch any flickers or sparkles? Are there any glints? Are there any animals near you? Do you feel any tinglings, touches or warm spots on any particular part of the body? Pay attention to everything you see, feel and hear.

Remember that the fire faeries and spirits are often the most difficult to recognize tangibly. Don't worry that you may be imagining it all. Imagination is not the same as unreality. Take a moment and give thanks to the element of fire and those beings in it for sharing with you. Give thanks and acknowledgment to your own personal salamander.

Breathe deeply of the sun or the fire and notice how it makes you feel now. Now go about your day's business, knowing that each time hereafter, the connections and the responses will grow even more dynamic.

Exercise #5:
Meeting the King of the Salamanders

1. Begin this meditation just as you did the previous exercise. Find a time and place outdoors, preferably, on a sunny day or where you can sit before a fire.

2. Now close your eyes and take several deep breaths to relax. Breathe in the sun. Know that with each breath you are aligning with the fire element more closely. Feel the atmosphere around you. Notice how the sun dances upon your face and body. Can you hear it as it caresses you? Now breathe deeply again of the sun's energy, and know that as you do you are calling forth your own personal salamander to help you in meeting the king of the fire element.

3. As you relax, begin to visualize the scene changing around you. You are standing at the base of a great volcano. The earth about you is charred and parched. Steam rises sporadically from cracks and fissures in the earth. The sun is strong

upon your face. The whole area appears parched and lifeless, but you are stimulated, and you know you would not
be so if there were no life here.

Although the sun is warm upon you, it is not uncomfortable. In fact, you find it powerful and stimulating. With each
breath, you seem to draw more of its energy into you—as if
you can draw it in and radiate it back out again.

As you breathe deeply, the earth trembles beneath your
feet. You raise your eyes to the mouth of the volcano above
you. Steam and flames erupt suddenly from it, filling the air
above with heat and light. The colors of the flames are intense—so strong that the sun is lost behind them. And then,
just as suddenly, all is still.

You are not afraid. Instinctively you know that in spite of
the activity, there is no danger. In fact, you are thrilled. And
you feel more alive than you have felt in ages.

Then again, the earth trembles beneath your feet. Some
of the fissures and cracks about you widen. Fire and steam
pours out from them. It is beautiful. You are amazed at the
play of the flames through the steam as it rises up, shifting
and dancing. And then you notice it seems to be moving toward you.

At first fearful of what its temperature might be, you are
surprised to find it warm and soothing. There is a powerful
gentleness to it that borders on the erotic but energizes you
on all levels. It is a fire that doesn't burn.

As it forms around you, the volcano disappears from
view, as does the sun. You are immersed in the swirling
steam and the dancing flames. And then it begins to change,
and as you peer through them, you see the vague outline of a
form. The flames and steam actually seem to be dancing
about it, as if it were the center of their life and activity.
Somehow you know that this must be Djinn, king of the element of fire.

You whisper his name—more to yourself than to him—
but the flames respond. You feel warm air rush over you, as
though being breathed upon. The flames and steam shift
even more. The figure becomes even more defined.

A second time you speak the name—this time louder,
bolder and directly to the form. The flames rise in response,

increasing their activity and giving forth more light. The steam shifts and begins to dissipate. The figure becomes even more distinct and even begins to move.

A third time you speak the name of Djinn. You sing it out loud and clear, passionately, as if you are becoming enflamed yourself. The steam parts, the flames rise and then disappear. Djinn steps forward to stand before you.

He is tall, and looks like the traditional genie of lore. He is dressed in brilliant reds and oranges, and you are sure you can see tiny flames dancing in his eyes. His face is passionate and strong, and the energy comes off him in waves, like heat rising from the road on a summer's day. Occasionally tiny flames leap up and then disappear around him.

He motions with his hand to follow him, and you feel a rush of warm air. He begins moving to the mouth of the volcano. You follow. At the edge, you look down and see the molten earth and fires in its heart.

Djinn reaches down and draws a tiny flame out from the volcano. He then takes one of your hands and holds it palm up. Your eyes widen, fearful of what the flame might do. You try to pull back, but his eyes fix yours and a wave of courage and strength fills your being. Your hand steadies, and you nod to him. He places the flame upon the palm of your hand.

You laugh, for it tickles. It doesn't burn at all. Djinn smiles briefly at your amazement and wonder as you watch the flame dance within your hand.

"Fire is essential to life. Yes, it can burn and destroy, but it also soothes and creates. You could not exist without fire, nor could anything upon this planet. Wherever life exists, fire also exists—from the heart of the planet to the heart of the human."

His voice is filled with great warmth and compassion. You expected one of such an element to speak with the force of great fires. You expected his energy to overwhelm you.

"When we learn to control our passions, we have control over that which we create. When we have no control over our passions, our inner fire, we are at the mercy of whatever fire may be burning. With no control, life plays you, rather than you playing it. The key to controlling the outcome of one's life is control of the fire elements. You must develop the courage to dance with it, burn the old with it and stimulate new birth."

Djinn takes the flame from the palm of your hand and drops it back into the volcano. As it touches the center, a ripple of flames spreads out from that point to form a circle of fire. In the midst, images begin to form.

You see the Earth and the sun and the force of its fire as essential to life upon Earth. You see the changes in seasons and how the raising and lowering of temperatures is a catalyst to stages of growth, for plants, animals and humans. Then you see yourself and the fires of your own metabolism. You see how vigorous physical exercise stimulates activity of the fire element within you. You see how it is tied to sexuality and eroticism—physical and mystical.

Then the images change. You see the passions you have had and did not act upon. You see those times you used your fires to show courage and strength—if only to fulfill the responsibilities of your life. You see the ideals you wished to explore, and you see where you stepped from them onto easier, safer paths.

The images shift again. You see times in which you expressed courage and succeeded. And you see yourself shining with fire at such times. You see the times you went through great changes and upheaval, and you see your own fires growing stronger to help you. You see the many times things have ended and people have left your life—taking with them some of your fire. And you see the many times new people and situations have arisen—stimulating new sparks and fire for you.

"Most never understand how to use my element. Fire gives courage and strength when there is no one else to depend on. Fire enables us to leave that which is no longer beneficial. Fire enables us to see new opportunities. Yes, fire destroys, but you can not have destruction without creation.

"Learning to work with fire is learning to follow your own passions and your own rhythms. Every fire burns unique to itself. It has its own dance pattern. It has its own rhythm. As you follow your own rhythms, your fires grow stronger and you find that that which did not work now will.

"As you learn to attune to the element of fire and those of us who work and live within it, your passion for life will increase. You will find your own personal rhythms for living, and you will find the courage to follow them. It is then that life takes on new light. And no matter what the ashes of your present life circumstances may be, you will rise from them like the phoenix."

From the center of that circle of flame, a single flame extends up. It shifts and stretches, rising into the air above the volcano. There you see it form the mythical bird of re-birth—the phoenix. Then it disappears.

Djinn extends his hand back into the molten lava of the volcano. As he withdraws it, you see he is holding a piece of flint. He places it within your hand, and as he does, flames and steam rise from all of the fissures around this volcano. The sun reflects off of it, and for a moment you are sure that flash of light off of the flint had a musical sound.

"This is a sign of my promise to work with you and help open the mysteries of fire to you. Fire is powerful, and many societies made sacrifices to gods and goddesses of this element. It burns while it heals, it destroys while it creates. It strengthens and impassions. By learning to work with it you will learn to bring your greatest passions into manifestation. You will learn what you must release in order to fulfill.

"It carries great responsibilities. If you accept this, your passions will grow. You will become catalytic in your own life but in the lives of others—for good or bad. You will learn to burn away the dross of your life to reveal the light of gold beneath. You will find the law of cause and effect manifesting more clearly and more rapidly—for good and bad. You will learn about physical and spiritual alchemy. Your old self will die, so that a new self may be born.

"If you are unsure of this commitment, leave the flint upon the edge of this volcano. Here it will always remain until such time as you choose to take it upon yourself. The choice is always yours."

The flames from the volcano rise up extending ten feet above. Djinn nods to you, and steps off the edge into the midst of the flames. They dance around him, growing stronger and brighter, and then they drop quickly down into the volcano itself. The only sign of Djinn is the warmth that rises from the lava.

You hold the piece of flint before you and examine it. You look at the flames of the inner volcano and the rays of the sun dancing off its edges. The act of striking flint to make fire is powerful and significant. You breathe deeply of the ethereal fires within the air about you. You make your decision, and the image of the volcano and the sun begins to fade. You find yourself back where you started at the beginning of this meditation.

∾❅

Excerpt From My Personal Journal

Again before starting work on the chapter with fire faeries, I performed my fire faerie meditation. As I began, a soft breeze filled my room. As I continued, I noticed the cessation of the breeze and the temperature in the room rising.

Throughout the day, the temperature would go up, and by noon the hot weather was back with temperatures in the upper nineties and humidity increasing as well. Occasionally I would look out my window to observe the work at hand behind my house.

The workers seemed to be taking more and more breaks because of the heat, but unfortunately the damage was done. Most of the trees had been taken out and the earth in that area looked like a desolate wasteland. How appropriate that the area takes on a desert appearance on the days I focus most strongly upon the fire spirits . . .

(Continued at the end of Chapter Ten)

~❧~

Chapter Eight

Finding the
Flower Faeries

In the midst of the garden grew a rosebush, which was quite covered with roses; and in one of them, the most beautiful of all, there dwelt an elf. He was so tiny that no human eye could see him. Behind every leaf in the rose he had a bedroom. He was as well-formed and as beautiful as any child could be, and he had wings that reached from his shoulders to his feet. Oh, what a fragrance there was in his rooms, and how clear and bright were the walls! They were made of the pale pink rose leaves.

The whole day he rejoiced in the warm sunshine, flew from flower to flower, danced on the wings of the flying butterfly, and measured how many steps he would have to take to pass along all the roads and crossroads that are marked out on a single hidden leaf. What we call veins on the leaf were to him high roads and crossroads ... *

Flower faeries and elves are some of the most delicate and beautiful of the faerie realm. They are as myriad as the flowers themselves, and they serve many functions in regard to the flowers.

---

* Hans Christian Andersen. "The Rose Elf," *The Complete Stories of Hans Christian Andersen*. Trans. by H.W. Dulcken. (London: Chancellor Press, 1983), p. 376.

There are faeries that help the flowers emit their fragrances. There are faeries that assist in making them grow. There are flower elves and gnomes who work to create the color of the flowers, and there are field faeries and elves who watch over the entire area in which they grow.

There is also for every single flower one particular faerie who embodies the spirit and essence of the flower itself. This faerie or elf often oversees the activities of the others working with and around that particular flower. Learning to connect with this faerie is the key to unlocking all of the energies of the flower and opening perception to all of the others working around it.

Flowers have always been great sources of inspiration and energy. All aspects of flowers have been used by healers, metaphysicians and poets. Many flowers have been associated with gods and goddesses and are often endowed with mystical qualities.

Flowers in any form are sources of strong energy vibrations. Even dried flowers continue to be such. It is only decayed and decaying flowers which do not. In the case of decayed and decaying flowers, the elementals work for the breakdown of the flower, to return it to its natural element. All of the energy of the elementals and the flower faeries in such cases are drawn inward to facilitate this breakdown. Thus the energy of the flowers in such states has an inverse energy effect. Instead of giving off energy, they draw it away.

Because of this, it is not beneficial to have decaying flowers indoors or in close proximity to you, as the elementals may draw on your energies to assist the breakdown of the flowers. You may feel energy drains and tiredness as a result. Flowers in the house that are decaying should be removed to an outdoor location (compost area, etc.). Wildflowers that are dying are usually no problem, as the elementals draw from the natural environment to assist the breakdown, and so you will feel little or no effects.

Modern spiritualists are very familiar with the energy aspects of flowers and flower faeries. They take care to set flowers in the seance room or any room in which spiritual activities are going to occur. The fragrance, color and activity of the flower faeries raise the energy vibrations of the individuals and the environment.

It is important to note that picking a flower does not stop the activities of the flower faeries and elementals. Part of the reason a rosebud will bloom even after it is picked is because of the continued work of the flower faeries.

As the flower dies however, so will the primary spirit of the flower, along with some of the other faeries associated with that flower. Some may move on to other flowers in that environment and work to assist them to grow. The elementals though remain to assist in the breakdown of the flower and its return to its natural elements. In the case of perennials, the flower faeries withdraw and help protect the plant through its dormant stages until it is time to sprout and blossom again.

There are many who find this very sad, but we must keep in mind that those of the faerie realm have a much better view of the life and death process than humans. They see it as a creative process, filled with joy on all levels. To the flower faeries and others of this realm who have short life spans, the time they have is one that is wonderfully bright, warm and beautiful. While we may have thousands of days, they have thousands of moments in which they rejoice in their life. They also know that beauty will not cease when they die. To them every moment of their life is long and beautiful, full of joy and sweet feeling.

Flower faeries speak to us often. Most of the time, we don't pay any attention. Have you ever been for a walk and caught the soft fragrance of a flower? The faeries have greeted you. Have you ever commented on the beautiful color of a particular flower? The faeries have caught your attention. Is there a particular flower that is your favorite? Its flower faeries have something special to share with you. Every time you inhale the sweet fragrance of a flower or comment upon its color, you acknowledge the flower faeries.

Every flower faerie and elf is a wonderfully unique creation. Each has its own energy, its own appearance and often its own personality. Each flower, and thus each flower faerie, can teach us something different. Every flower and faerie will interact with us in their own unique way. Every flower faerie has its own wisdom that they will joyfully share with us if we are open.

It is not difficult to attune to the flower faeries. Begin by learning as much about flowers as possible. How and where do they grow? Learn about their growing processes and all of their parts: roots, bulbs, stems, leaves, blossoms, etc. Every aspect of the flower means something and is tied to some faerie activity.

Buy bouquets of flowers on a regular basis. Paint and draw pictures of them. Plant them in your yard, house or garden. Have an area of your yard in which you allow wildflowers to grow freely. Make an amulet that has a picture of your favorite flower on one side and a picture of the faerie on the other. Use the meditation at the end of this chapter on a regular basis; it will increase your connection to the flower faeries immensely.

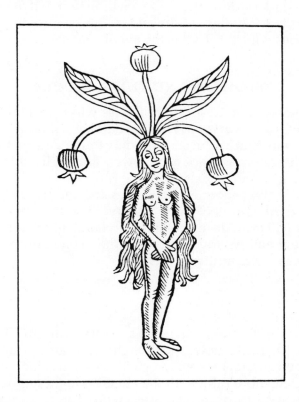

By aligning yourself with the flower faeries and elves, you align yourself with one of the most creative expressions of Mother Nature herself. You open yourself to creation, joy, growth and sustenance. It is these qualities of Mother Nature that are symbolized by all flowers and epitomized by the flower faeries and elves.

The following list of flowers contains information about the faeries and elves associated with them. It also includes the wisdom and energy they can easily impart to us, if we learn to work with them. Remember that each flower and its faeries are unique to themselves, but certain groups of flowers and their faeries embody specific characteristics.

The information given is what I have uncovered from my explorations and research into the flowers themselves and my meditations with their flower faeries. If you have always been drawn to specific flowers, examine them first. The descriptions may provide insight into why you have been drawn to them. You will learn how the faeries work through them. Do not limit yourself to my descriptions. Use the meditation at the end of this chapter to open to the flower faeries yourself. That is the joy of discovery.

FLOWERS AND THEIR FAERIES

Remember that most flower faeries will reveal themselves in the colors of the flower itself. The flowers I have chosen to use in this section are ones that are most commonly found and are the most accessible. There is a vast variety of flowers and each has its own faeries and energies.

Many healing energies, properties and symbolic significances of flowers are the result of faerie activity. Exploring those aspects of any flower will provide insight into the character of the faeries associated with them. As you learn to attune to one flower faerie, you will find it easier to attune to them all.

Angelica

The flower faeries of angelica are very beautiful. The plant is from the wild carrot family, and though many see it as not that beautiful, the faeries and elves belie such impressions. For anyone wishing to connect more fully with the angelic kingdom, this is a wonderful flower to learn to commune with. The faeries of angelica strengthen the aura and they bring good fortune and strong energy. They hold the knowledge of how to radiate more joy in all circumstances. They can reveal the nature and cause of problems in your life. They will stimulate intuition, and they will even leave the flower and follow individuals they are attracted to for brief periods, serving as friends and temporary guardians.

Basil

The faerie spirit of basil often shows itself in more of an elf form. It holds the knowledge of integrating sexuality and spirituality. Wherever basil grows, there is usually a dragon to be found in that same environment, serving as protector. It also draws dragons when burned as an incense. The faeries and spirits of basil help us awaken greater discipline and devotion.

Black-Eyed Susan

The faerie of this flower can become a wonderful catalyst for change. It often has tremendous insight into the emotional aspects of those who come in touch with it. It can help shed light on dark areas of the soul. These faeries can show how to make the proper changes.

Buttercup

This flower faerie is so compassionate and so empathic towards humans that it will help you come to know your own special gifts and how to apply them in this lifetime. This flower and its faeries bring tremendous healing energies and great understanding of the human condition. Because of this, they are beneficial in helping us rediscover our self-worth. They can shed light on opening to new opportunities and new life directions.

Carnation

The flower faeries of the carnation will take the color of the flower itself. They radiate strong feelings of deep love for humans. Their energy is healing to the entire body. Their fragrance and color are tools by which they provide their healings. Contact with them strengthens the aura and restores a love of self and life.

Chrysanthemum

The flower faeries of mums easily touch the heart. They stimulate vitality, and they can help strengthen the overall life force of the individual. They hold knowledge of how to express one's life force more lovingly as a healing force.

Clover

The faeries of clover often have an elfin quality about them. It is not unusual to find the occasional leprechaun somewhere in a field of clover. The clover faeries assist in finding love and fidelity. They can aid in developing psychic abilities. The clover faeries reveal themselves readily to individuals who display kindness toward nature. They often first show themselves through flickering lights around the clover itself. The faeries of white clover are most power-ful and apparent around the time of the full moon.

Ordinary water can become enchanted by infusing it with clo-ver found at the favorite haunts of faeries. Washing the eyes with this water can awaken sight of the closest faeries.

Coleus

The flower faeries of the coleus have a strong effect upon our feminine energies. They can awaken the innate healing energies of the individual. They can stimulate vision of a new spiritual path—one that will enable you to draw upon your own beauty and power. The coleus flower faeries reveal themselves most readily to those who have ties—real or symbolic, magical or mythical—to the Ar-thurian legends and the beings associated with it.

Daffodil

The faeries of this flower can help us to realize our own inner beauty. They are beneficial in teaching us how to achieve deeper levels of meditation, and they bring greater clarity of thought. These faeries always have a wonderful glow about them that causes us to see ourselves in a new light.

Daisy

This flower is drawing to all faeries, elves and nature spirits. Where it is found, nature spirits, even those not associated with the flower, will also be found. It is one of the best flowers to work with to begin communion with the faerie kingdom, as its faeries have no fear of humans and are very open to contact. They stimulate great physical awareness of the presence of nature spirits. The daisy is a favorite flower of dryads (wood nymphs), and simply sitting among the flowers invites contact. Daisy faeries help awaken crea-tivity and inner strength.

Faerie Lantern

The energies of the faeries around this flower are very strong. It is important when working with this flower to stay grounded, as you may find yourself becoming "faerie charmed." They have a strong effect upon the imagination, and they are wonderful to work with for anyone wishing to re-awaken or reconnect with the inner child. They awaken the feminine energies that are strong in all prepubescent children. They hold knowledge of re-awakening and re-expression of sexual energies.

Gardenia

Faeries of this flower hold knowledge of telepathy. They can help us increase telepathic abilities with all of the nature spirits. They stimulate feelings of peace, and occasionally the faerie spirit of this flower will follow individuals around for brief periods to raise the spirits and provide protection. These flower faeries are very protective toward children, and it is beneficial to have them growing in areas where children play.

Geranium

The faeries and elves of this flower awaken a sense of happiness and stir the heart chakra. In most geranium beds will be found an elf who oversees the entire area. The faeries of this flower strengthen and vitalize the aura. They also can show you where you may be missing opportunities for happiness.

Heather

In the bloom of the heather are faeries that have a unique ability to stimulate greater self-expression. They are especially drawn and open to those children and adults who are shy and introverted. They can facilitate outward expression and the manifesting of inner abilities. This is a bloom that seems to have a number of faerie spirits that oversee its growth, rather than just one. This may be due to the fact that it is sometimes considered a tree, although I have never seen a tree spirit with it—only the flower faeries.

Honeysuckle

The flower faeries and elves of honeysuckle are powerful. They hold much knowledge about aromatherapy, especially in overcoming the past. Contact with them often stimulates powerful dreams, and they awaken greater psychic energy. They can teach how to develop your own charms and "glamour" so that others are more drawn to you.

Hyacinth

Attuning to the faeries of this fragrant flower is like attuning to a sweet song of youth—a song that restores belief that all is possible. These faeries hold many answers to the mysteries of death and burial, and they have an energy that can help overcome grief. Their energy awakens greater gentleness, and they can teach how to use gentleness as a dynamic power.

Iris

Iris was the Greek goddess of the rainbow, and the faeries of this flower manifest in all of the colors of the rainbow itself. These faeries can open the entire faerie realm to your vision. They stimulate great inspiration, creative expression and psychic purity. They bring to the auric field a strong sense of peace and the hope for new birth.

Jasmine

This flower was sacred in Persia. The faeries and spirits associated with it are both ancient and wise. The faeries of the individual flowers are linked to ancient devas who oversaw the mystery schools of ancient Persia. They hold the key to using dreams for prophecy. They can help develop discrimination and mental clarity. When going through major transitions, one can do no better than to connect with the faeries of this flower.

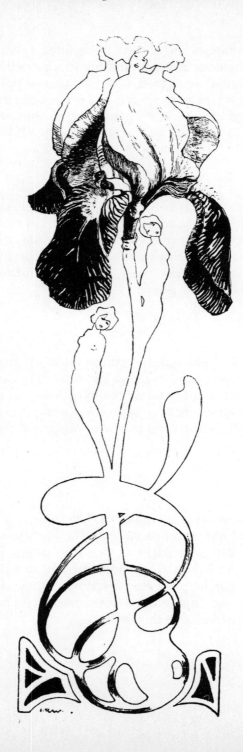

Lavender

As an herb, lavender has been responsible for many healing and magical properties. Much of this is due to the strong activity of the faeries surrounding it. Wherever lavender grows, there will always be great faerie and elf activity—and not just associated with the plant itself. The faeries of lavender can help you to open physical vision of nature spirits. One of the most powerful times to connect with them is on Midsummer Eve.

The faeries of this flower and the other nature spirits it draws are very protective. There are many faerie tales about individuals who suffered cruel treatment by spouses, and as a result incurred some problems themselves. The faeries of lavender can bring healing and protection, and they can assist us in overcoming emotional blocks.

Lilac

Although technically a tree, the blossoms of the lilac are filled with faerie and elf activity. The flower is very fragrant and powerful, and as you learn to attune to the nature spirits associated with it, you will find the fragrance also has a musical harmony to it. The faeries of this flower are musical in their communications. They can help harmonize our life and activate greater clairvoyance. They also can reveal to you past lives and how they are harmonized with your present.

Lily

The activity of the faeries of this flower are most powerfully connected to during the winter, but especially at the winter solstice. This flower is a favorite of the nature spirits, probably because it has links to the archangel Gabriel. These faeries can help connect you with the mysteries of new birth. They help in the development of purity and humility.

Marigold

The faeries and nature spirits associated with this flower can help you to develop clairaudience. You will find that as you begin to attune to them, you will start actually hearing them. They hold the mysteries and magic of thunderstorms. They also hold great knowledge of the power of words—especially when used in the healing process. They have knowledge of the mysteries of love and sacrifice.

Orchid

Wherever orchids grow, you will find nature spirits, elves, faeries and even some of the fantastic creatures and beings associated with the faerie realm. This flower was named for a nymph who was seduced by a satyr, and thus this flower and its environment is often watched over by nymphs and/or satyrs. These spirits have a dynamic effect upon sexual energy, and they have knowledge of the spiritual aspects of sexuality, as well as techniques of sex magic. Their energy is strong and it often affects the sexual drive.

Phlox

The spirit of phlox often takes the elf form, although there are many phlox faeries. The elf spirit seems to be more of an overseer and guardian. This is not its only form, but it is one that is most commonly experienced. The phlox elf can help you awaken latent artistic energies, and it is not unusual to find them occasionally taking up residence in a house to assist in the development of skill or craftsmanship in some area. Attuning to the beings of this flower can assist you in becoming more productive in your life.

Poppy

Used as a flower essence, it makes you more perceptive to encounters with the various beings of the faerie realm and facilitates visions of the subtle energies of life.

Rose

One of the most sacred flowers, the faeries and spirits of it have strong ties to their elder brothers and sisters, the angels. Attuning to them can help you awaken a greater sense of love, as well as attunement to the angelic hierarchy. They can teach the crafts of telepathy and divination. They hold the secrets to time and its exploration. The faerie of the white rose can help us develop spiritual purity and awaken our own divinity. The faerie of the red rose can assist us in all aspects of love and fertility. The pink rose faerie can teach us how to blend the male and female for new birth. The yellow rose faerie can teach us how to recognize and express truth.

Rosemary

This herb has a long history associated with elves and faeries. Sprigs of it are hung on Christmas trees in England as an offering and expression of gratitude to the elves for their assistance throughout the year. The faeries and beings of the rosemary plant were often used to help combat any form of black magic or hatred. Their energy is very powerful and positive. They stimulate clarity of mind and creativity. They can also help teach and facilitate out-of-body experiences.

Sage

The faeries and elves of sage have great energy, and just being around the plant can induce light altered states of consciousness. Attuning to them can help you facilitate mediumistic abilities. They have knowledge of how to slow the aging process, and they can awaken a newfound sense of immortality and wisdom within your life. They also stimulate an increased interest in spiritual matters.

Snapdragon

Just like its name, this plant and the environment in which it grows are often watched over by tiny etheric dragons. The spirits of this flower have connections to the energies of all dragons. They can help you open the throat chakra, stimulating your own will force and creative expression. They can help you develop clairaudience. It is not unusual for those who learn to attune to the snapdragon beings to begin hearing spirits with increasing frequency. These beings bring great protection.

Thyme

When used as a bedtime fragrance, thyme draws the wee folk into your sleeping chambers.

Tulip

Inside the cup of the tulip sits a beautiful flower faerie. This beautiful being awakens trust and helps to clear the mental faculties. These flower faeries can stimulate greater vision, and they hold knowledge of the hidden significance of events, people and things.

Violet

The violet is the flower of simplicity and modesty, two of the best qualities to develop in attuning to faeries and elves. The violet is sacred to all faeries, especially the faerie queen. Gathering the first violet in the spring invites the energy of luck and assistance of the faerie realm into your life for the fulfillment of a wish in the year ahead. The individual violet faeries can help you discern your relationship within groups. They awaken greater psychic sensitivity, and they often reveal themselves through dreams.

Exercise:
Meeting the Flower Faeries

This meditation can be adapted and used to attune to all flower faeries. It can be performed outside in the midst of a flower bed, or it can be performed inside while holding an individual flower upon your lap. When I perform one of my workshops on faeries and elves, I bring to the class a dozen or so different kinds of fresh cut flowers, making sure I have enough for everyone in attendance. In this way each can choose the flower he or she is drawn to—the one in which the flower faerie speaks the loudest.

1. Choose a time in which you will not be disturbed. This exercise is most effective when performed outdoors, but it is not essential. When performed indoors, use a fresh cut flower and have it in your hand or on your lap.

2. You may wish to perform a progressive relaxation. You may also wish to use some music in the background. All faeries and elves are drawn to music. In the appendix are some pieces of music that are beneficial to drawing the faeries and elves out more effectively. You may simply want to use sound effects of the outdoors.

3. Take time to examine the flower. Become familiar with it. Take note of its color, stem and shape. Touch its petals. Caress your cheek with it. How does it feel? Bring the flower up to your nose and inhale its fragrance. Note how it makes you feel.

4. Close your eyes and breathe deeply. Allow yourself to relax. Bring the flower up to your nose and inhale its fragrance again, and then allow the flower to rest on your lap. As you focus on the fragrance, visualize yourself sitting in a beautiful garden.

   All around you are flowers and trees. The grass beneath you is soft and lush. The air is fresh and clean. The sunlight that penetrates the trees to touch this garden is soft and muted, casting the area in soft haze. You are relaxed and at peace.

   You know this place. You have seen it before. Maybe it was in your dreams or maybe in a distant lifetime—it doesn't matter. Somehow you know that this is a place where you can go to heal and refresh yourself. It is a place where all worlds meet.

   In the distance is a high mountain and a path leading up to it. The path is lined with trees and stones of every color. On the opposite side of this garden is another path, leading from the garden to a valley below. As you look down this path, you see your present home.

   You understand that you are at an intersection of time and place. It is an inner sanctuary where the real and the imagined meet. It is a place of the finite and the infinite, the physical and the ethereal.

   It is then that you notice the flower on your lap. It seems to shine, and as you focus on it a soft, pleasing sound is heard. It is as if there were a tiny voice singing.

You bring the flower to your nose and inhale its fragrance, and it makes you lightheaded and you smile because it is so pleasant. As you gaze at the beauty of this flower, the petals begin to unfold. One by one, each petal unfolds, and as it does the music grows more distinct.

As the flower blossoms before your eyes, you see in its heart a soft ball of light, the color of the flower itself. Pastel and shimmering, it seems to float upon the flower petals. Then it shifts, changing forms before your eyes. As it does you are filled with wonder. It almost seems to make your own heart sing.

And then you hear your name whispered from that light, and it shimmers once more. Before you now lights a tiny beautiful faerie. Its eyes are filled with joy and love, as if it had been waiting for you for a long time.

As it shimmers and dances before you, you hear it singing within your own mind. Its voice is soft and has a musical quality to it. You are not sure how it is doing it, but you can hear its every thought. It laughs lightly at your amazement.

Then it begins to speak. It tells you of its activity. It speaks of its purpose. It tells you what it will share with you if you work with nature. It tells you of the mystery of the flower and why this one is important to you now.

You are filled with delight. And though a tiny being, its energy as it speaks in your mind sends shivers of delight throughout your body and soul. You gently hold out your hand, and it flies from the flower to your palm, showing you its trust. And then it returns to the flower again.

It begins to shimmer and dance, becoming more vague. And you hear in your mind the promise: "Next time, we will share more." Then as the petals of the flower begin to fold up, the faerie becomes a soft ball of light within its heart. Though the flower has closed up, you can still hear its sweet song.

You raise the flower to your nose, and inhale its fragrance. You brush its petals lightly against your cheek. As you do, you notice the garden scene around you fading, becoming indistinct.

Breathe deeply and feel yourself relaxed. You are sitting where you started, comfortable and peaceful. You remember all that you have experienced, and you now know why you were drawn to this flower. Slowly and gently you open your eyes and gaze upon the flower in your lap. For perhaps the first time you are truly aware of the life and energy within nature that surrounds you.

5. At this point you might want to ground yourself by taking a walk in nature. You may wish to give thanks to the flower faerie for sharing with you. You may even wish to record what you experienced. One way of honoring this meeting and all meetings in the future is to plant some flowers or buy a plant that you can take care of in your home.

 ✧

Chapter Nine

The Touch
of the Tree Spirits

The tree is an ancient magical symbol. It represents all things that grow, fertility and life itself. To some it is the world axis, to others it is the world itself. Its roots are in the earth, and yet its branches reach toward the heavens. It is a bridge between heaven and earth, a mediator between the two worlds. It is a natural doorway to other realms, especially that of the faeries and elves.

The tree has been associated with both paradise and hell—the Tree of Life and the Tree of Knowledge. In Greek mythology the Golden Fleece hung upon a tree. The Christian cross was originally a tree. Buddha found enlightenment sitting under one. Odin hung upon the great tree Yggdrasil for nine days and nights in order to attain higher wisdom. The ancient Druids recognized distinct energies of individual trees. Every civilization has its stories, myths and legends of the tree.

Consider too all that is done with trees. They bear fruit, they provide wood, shade, windbreaks and shelters. They are boundaries, separating one piece of land from another or one world from another. Every tree can be a doorway to the faerie realm.

All children are drawn to them. They climb them, play in them and even build houses in them. Much of this has to do with the energy of the tree and its connection to the faerie realm. Children are drawn naturally to those places where faeries are found; and faeries and elves are drawn to children, stimulating imagination and play in them. Children instinctively feel the spirit of trees, even if they do not recognize it for what it is.

Trees have always been imbued with certain magical and spiritual attributes. Our superstition of "knocking on wood" was initiated to insure that no spirits were residing within the tree before it was cut down. In German folklore, one particular group of spirits, known as the kobold, inhabited trees. The trees in which these sprites lived were cut down and sections were carved into figures so that the sprites would still have a home. They were then enclosed in wooden boxes and brought inside the home. The children were warned never to go near them. If they opened a box, the kobold would be released and wreak havoc. The jack-in-the-box was designed to scare children away so that the kobold would not be disturbed again.

No tree is without its spirit. It is home to a living being that oversees all activities and energies associated with the tree. This spirit grows with the tree and disappears with its death.

Tree spirits have great dignity. Tree spirits are generally affectionate to people, and are drawn to humans. It is not unusual for humans to have their favorite tree and for trees to have their favorite human.

I was always very fortunate to have had close contact with a wide variety of trees. Most of my early life was spent in an area in which there was an abundance of woods. My brothers and I played in the woods, among the trees, creeks and ponds. My grandfather would occasionally walk in the woods, looking for young trees to transplant to our yard. When he walked, his head would always be cocked as if listening, and then he would just suddenly stop and know exactly which tree to take.

One of the first tree spirits I ever truly encountered was an elm in a part of the woods where we often played tag, hide-and-seek and other games. I remember one time hiding next to an elm, behind a bush at its base. The bush was sparse, I knew if someone came by that I would be spotted. And yet I couldn't move either, for that would surely give me away. I could hear the others drawing close, and I didn't know what to do.

It was then that I heard a soft voice whisper my name. I jumped, startled at first, and then heard a soft, gentle laugh. I raised my head to the branches above me, following the sound of the laughter. I saw a soft face appear in the bark.

"Just lean back against me," the tree whispered, "and imagine that you are part of my bark."

I was stunned, but I leaned back, making myself comfortable. I heard my brothers' voices and the voices of our friends. I was the only one who had not been found. They drew closer, and I could hear them scouring the bushes for me.

I found myself relaxing, and at times I felt like I was sinking into the tree itself. I even felt like I was peering out from the bark, just like the face I had seen when I heard my name. I even felt a little sleepy, but I fought it. I was afraid that if I fell asleep, I would be found.

They searched all around for me. One of my brothers and one of our friends even stood not six inches from me, and I knew that I was invisible to them. I remember having to stifle a giggle. As they moved off to another part of the woods, I felt myself sitting outside the bark again.

I stood and faced the tree, unsure what to say or do. The face within it was very distinct, and it smiled and again laughed softly. It was the beginning of a wonderful friendship. I would go back to that tree many times to hide, and never was I ever caught there. This beautiful spirit would show me how to see spirits in trees and plants and how to become one with them. I didn't know it then, but I was receiving my first lessons in shape-shifting.

Tree spirits are not bound to the tree, although they will often stay close. They can emerge from the tree for a little distance when they desire. Usually, during the day, they are so busy with normal growing activities, they are not as discernible. At night, when the outside world slows down, they are more free. They have greater opportunity to move about. Many people get jitters when outside at night, especially in forested and wooded areas. Part of this is a response to the energy of the tree spirits as they begin to emerge from the trees and their presence is felt more strongly.

They are not harmful, but they are drawn to humans. They can also be quite affectionate. It is easier to feel their presence when the day's activities have slowed. They often have vibrations that are so strong and different that people will get chills and shivers when they are around.

Every tree is also home to a wide variety of elves and faeries. Often these live in communities and are seen in groups. Many of them are tied to the tree for life, and thus they are very protective of them. It is also why it is best to ask their permission before cutting.

The tree elves are usually what are first seen by humans around the tree, and are often mistaken for the actual tree spirit. Most of these faeries and elves are earth spirits. Thy often live beneath the surface of the tree, but they are frequently seen running along its branches. A great horned owl appearing in an oak tree can often be a signal of the presence of a shape-shifting wood elf.

The elder tree has the highest elf population. Under its roots live many tiny elves. The elder also has its own faerie personality, sheltering many good elves and faeries. The oak tree has a long history of magic and faerie lore associated with it. It is often the home or gathering spot of many nature spirits, and it always resents being cut. Elms will mourn cut members of their family, and willow spirits have been known to follow travelers on dark nights for short distances, muttering behind them. The hawthorn has long been considered an elf tree, and cutting one will bring misfortune from the elves that lived within it. The lime tree in Denmark is thought to be a favorite of elves.

One group of elves found beneath trees are known as the moss maidens in Germanic lore. These very ancient beings live within the root systems of trees. They hold the knowledge of the healing power of all plants.

Actual tree faeries are rare, but many faeries will attach themselves to a particular tree or species of tree. Wildflowers when found at the base of a tree (especially the oak) often signal the homes of tiny faeries. The wildflowers grow at the foot of trees so they can share in the protection and energy of the tree spirit. The most common wildflower homes for tree faeries are cowslips, thyme, foxglove and bluebells.

There are others of the faerie realm who also gather and live around trees, in woods and forested areas. To the Greeks, they were known as dryads. To most people they are simply known as wood nymphs. They are still found in wooded and forested areas—especially those that are somewhat wild.

The wood nymphs are usually female, and wear little or no clothing. Glimpses usually show them as dancing in the sunlight that comes through the trees. They sing beautifully, often imitating the birds. They understand the language of animals and of humans. They have a great curiosity about humans, and although they usually avoid direct contact, they will risk it for the opportunity to observe humans.

Sometimes the wood nymphs will appear childlike, and they are drawn to certain kinds of trees. They are very playful and rejoice in all expressions of nature in their environment. In an area of the woods where I grew up that we called "Fort Apache" was a young wood nymph, although I did not realize it at the time. It was a young girl who always had a squirrel at her feet. I would see her occasionally spying on us through the trees while we played.

Once when I went to that area by myself, she came from behind the trees. She did not speak a lot, and she often laughed at my expressions, but never in a mean way. Her laugh was contagious, and

she let me pet her squirrel. She had a knack for avoiding my questions. She would just laugh when I asked her why I never saw her at school. Her answer to my question as to where she lived was always the same: "Around here." When I asked her name, she would pretend she didn't hear. To this day, I still do not know what her name was. Whenever she seemed tired of my questions, she would erupt with wonderful laughter and then run in among the trees, disappearing.

I remember the last time I saw her. I had gone to that area alone again. I wasn't sure if I would see her or not, as her appearances were becoming more and more scarce. I found her sitting by the creek with her feet in the water. She was crying. The squirrel was not with her, which I found to be very curious. I stood there, feeling awkward and wishing that I hadn't come out looking for her.

She looked up and gave me a half smile, as if she had heard my thoughts. I asked if she were all right, and she stood and said she was.

"Why are you crying?" I asked.

"I have to leave," she answered softly.

I remember shivering as the trees rustled with a sudden breeze. She stepped up to me and kissed me on the cheek. I was surprised. She laughed at my expression and then dashed off among the trees. I heard her call out, "I will remember you, Ted Andrews."

And then she was gone. I never saw her again. The next week, developers started clearing the area to build some new houses.

Along with the wood nymphs that are found within forested and heavily wooded areas, there is usually a mistress or lady of the woods. Often in the form of a beautiful woman, this spirit is guardian to entire forested areas or even small groves of trees. Birch groves are intersections in which they often appear.

These beings are enchantingly beautiful, and they speak the language of the animals. They are often tending to and tended by deer, and they sing sweet songs that touch the heart and bless the grove. They know all that goes on within their woods, and you only see them if they allow it—no matter how accidental it may seem. To encounter the lady of the woods is a blessing that is similar to those of the traditional faerie patrons and godmothers, as will be discussed in Chapter Eleven.

Facility at seeing the tree spirits and elves will vary from individual to individual. Much depends on practice and knowledge of what to look for. The meditation at the end of this chapter will help. Learning and studying about the qualities of the particular tree will also tell you a lot about the character of its spirit. The next section of this chapter will help you attune to some of the tree personalities and characteristics.

The following are general suggestions for attuning to tree spirits, faeries and elves:

1. Read and study the lore of trees.

2. Spend time around trees. Go to parks. Climb a tree or sit under them and just enjoy being in their presence.

3. If possible, take time to go out into nature on camping trips or extended outings—away from the city.

4. Meditate upon different trees. Pay attention to how each tree makes you feel. Try to determine its inner character and spirit. (Use the meditation at the end of this chapter to help.)

5. Occasionally sit at a distance from trees and bushes and then allow your eyes to half-focus, using a daydream kind of gaze upon the tree. Can you see any forms or faces in the configurations of bark and branches?

    Don't worry whether you may be imagining it. You are stretching your perceptions. This soft focus helps in seeing the spirit of the tree. It will usually be first noticed peering out from the gnarled bark. With practice and persistence, you will start to see much more.

TREES AND THEIR SPIRITS

Any tree can be a doorway into the faerie realm. Any tree can be a source of energy and creativity in its own way. By opening to those spirits, faeries and elves associated with the trees, we invoke the energy of the tree itself into our life.

Each tree and each tree spirit has its own unique qualities. Many of these are characterized by the various elves and spirits that surround it. These beings can help us in many areas of our lives. If patient, tree spirits will share their energy and their knowledge.

The following list is by no means complete. It is provided only to give you a starting point in recognizing, understanding and working with the energies of the various tree spirits. As you will see, some of these trees are also connected to fantastic creatures that are associated with the faerie realm (i.e. the phoenix, dragons, unicorns, etc.). Learning to attune to the spirit of the tree will help you connect with and understand the role and energies of them as well.

There is much that we can learn from every tree if we learn to feel the loving caress of the shade it provides and hear its soft whispers in the rustling of its leaves.

Alder

The spirit of the alder tree is very protective, and it has great knowledge about prophetic scrying with the use of water and mirrors. When it leaves the tree, it will often take the form of a raven.

Apple

The apple tree has many magical faerie characteristics associated with it. It is home to one of the fantastic creatures found within the faerie realm—the unicorn. Traditionally, the unicorn lives beneath the apple tree. The apple blossoms draw out great numbers of flower faeries in the spring who promote feelings of happiness in those who are near. The spirit of this tree holds the knowledge of eternal youth and beauty. Its spirit will often take the form of a beautifully enticing woman who can open the heart to new love.

Ash

The ash tree has great mysticism and power associated with it. In the Norse tradition, it was called Yggdrasil, the great tree of life. It is a doorway to many dimensions of the faerie realm. Its spirit is strong and holds the knowledge of how events and people are linked together. It can teach the magic of poetry and how to weave words into powerful effects.

Birch

The birch is a magical tree, and its spirit can connect you to many aspects of the elemental realms of life. It has a great antiquity, and it is sometimes known as the "lady of the woods." It is a doorway whose energy can connect you with all of the beings and goddesses of the woodlands (including the wood nymphs). The bark should never be taken without permission, but once achieved this wondrous spirit can demonstrate how to use a staff made from birch to pass from the mortal realm to the faerie realm and back again.

Cedar

This tree and its spirit are both protective and healing. It also has ties to the unicorn of the faerie realm—as the unicorn keeps its treasures in boxes made of cedar. This spirit brings calm and balance to emotions and can stimulate inspiring dream activity.

Cherry

Just as the apple tree is the home of the unicorn, the cherry tree is home to yet another of those fantastic creatures of the faerie realm—the phoenix. The spirit of this tree is often fiery in appearance. It has the ability to bring individuals to the threshold of a new awakening.

Elder

The elder tree was sacred to those of the Druid and Celtic traditions. It was the tree of birth and death, beginning and end. Its spirit is that of transition. It teaches how to awaken opportunity to cast out the old and build the new. This tree can be a doorway to link with the mother goddess in many forms.

This tree's spirit has knowledge of great magic. She can provide protection and add power to even the slightest of wishes. The elder spirit facilitates contact with all the beings of the woods, including the dryads and other wood nymphs. She is the mother who protects her groves and all of her children within them. It is the ideal tree spirit to connect with to awaken a renaissance with the faerie realm.

Elm

The elm is the tree of intuition. Its spirit holds knowledge of how to awaken it to its fullest. It can teach how to hear the "inner call." There is always great elf activity around this tree, so much so that if balance is not used, it is easy to become faerie charmed. This tree's spirit is so sensitive that it will mourn when other members of its family are cut down. It holds knowledge of empathy and compassion.

Hawthorn

The hawthorn is sacred to the faeries and elves. They hold great love for this tree and its spirit. This is the tree of magic—all of the magic found within the faerie realm. This spirit will provide a doorway to the inner realms, as well as protection against their magic. You must learn to be patient with the hawthorn spirit or those inner realm doors will not be opened to their fullest. This spirit can stimulate growth and fertility in all areas of your life, making it seem enchanted to others.

Hazel

This tree is home to a quiet spirit of magic. All fruit and nut trees are symbolic of hidden wisdom, and the spirit of this tree can help you acquire hidden wisdom in a unique manner. It will awaken the intuition and insight, and it holds knowledge of the electromagnetic fields of the Earth. Attuning to this spirit can reveal much information about dowsing. This quiet spirit also holds knowledge of the weaving of words for great effects, and it can teach how to go within the quiet of one's own mind and consciousness (meditation).

Holly

Technically, holly is a bush, but it has the power of a tree, and its spirit is often guardian to many of the "little people." The holly is home to great numbers of elves and faeries. It was sacred to the Druids who kept it inside their homes during the winter to provide a haven for the faerie beings. Its spirit often is seen in masculine form, and it has knowledge of the angelic realms and how to connect more fully. It can show how best to become a true spiritual warrior, and if worked with, it can stimulate dynamic healing abilities.

Maple

This is a spirit who always appears in its true androgynous form—neither male nor female, embodying qualities of both. It has great knowledge of balance and how to use balance to stay connected to Mother Earth. It can awaken the feminine aspects of nurturing, intuition and creativity. The flowering maple draws many faeries to it, and if attuned to during that time, the faeries will assist you in fulfilling sweet promises and aspirations.

Oak

The oak tree was sacred to the Celts and the Druids. It is home to a powerful spirit, which has great strength and endurance. It holds the ancient knowledge of the continuity of life, and just being near it is strengthening to the entire auric field. It is a natural doorway to the faerie realms and their mysteries. Every acorn has its own little faerie, and bringing an acorn into your home is a way of inviting more intimate contact with the faeries for brief periods. The oak tree is always home to great populations of elves and faeries.

The oak tree in which mistletoe is found is even more magical and powerful. Mistletoe, although found in the masculine oak, has faeries associated with it that embody the feminine energies. Where mistletoe is found, there will be faerie protection of children and those who are reconnecting with the child within. The faeries of the mistletoe hold the knowledge of invisibility and shape-shifting. They have great beauty and can stimulate fertility. Linking with mistletoe of the oak can awaken visions of your soul in the future.

Pine

The pine tree has a powerful and ancient spirit. It has ties to the Dionysian mysteries, and it was the sacred tree of Mithra. It was also sacred to Poseidon. Pine trees found along shorelines are often gathering spots for water spirits and sprites. This tree's spirit is healing and balancing, especially to emotions. It can show how to express our creative energies without feelings of guilt. It is protective against all forms of negativity.

Redwood

The redwood tree is one of the oldest and largest of the tree spirits upon the planet. They are direct descendants from the time known as Lemuria. They are homes to wondrous faeries and elves who, in spite of their rarity, are not shy about human contact. The redwood spirit can open great spiritual vision, and contact with them will bring extended growth periods that will touch the soul on many levels. They can help clarify one's own personal vision of life.

Rowan

The rowan is another ancient and magical tree. Its spirit holds the knowledge of the omens of nature and how to read them without becoming superstitious. This spirit is protective and visionary, and it can be used to connect with all goddesses. The wisdom of this spirit is so strong that when linked with, it can teach you to call up magic spirits, guides and elementals. It is a tree spirit who helps prevent intrusions by outside forces. It is grounding and prevents becoming lost in the faerie realms.

Spruce

The spirit of the spruce tree holds great knowledge about healing, especially in relation to the metaphysical causes of disease. Its spirit is gentle and will open the doorways to the faerie realm in the manner best handled by the individual. It is not unusual for those who attune to the spirit of spruce to find that there follows an increase in animals within that environment. The spruce spirit loves human company and activity, and it likes to align itself with families. If there is a spruce tree in the yard, it is often the primary protector and caretaker of the yard. It enjoys having a relationship with humans. The spruce spirit often affects the dream state and when attuned to will appear occasionally in them.

Sycamore

The sycamore was a sacred tree to the Egyptians and is still a doorway into those realms where beings and forces associated with Egypt can still be connected with. It can teach how to receive from the universe—be it in the form of assistance, compliments, or any other form. It holds the knowledge of the laws of abundance and supply and how to utilize them to your greatest benefit. It also has knowledge of hidden treasures. Attuning to the sycamore will augment all connections to nature.

Walnut

The walnut tree has an ancient spirit with knowledge of the tides of change. How to recognize and use them is part of what it can teach. It can open the individual to new perspectives on life. The walnut spirit also has knowledge of the mysteries of death and rebirth and how to apply them specifically to your life. It is a doorway into the faerie realm that can initiate change and the creative transition of rebirth. It also draws and houses faeries, and it is not unusual to find faeries gathering and playing upon the walnuts themselves.

Willow

The willow is a magical tree with great mysticism and life to it. It was associated with Orpheus in the Greek tradition and the goddess Brigid in the Celtic. It has a long association with the faerie realm. Its spirit and the elves who live under it are keepers of the knowledge of herbology. The willow tree can speak audibly to us, if we learn to quiet ourselves and listen. It is most discernible at night. The willow spirit often left the tree at night and followed travelers, muttering and speaking to them. Not understanding, most travelers were frightened by this. The willow spirit has knowledge of how to make and use magic wands. The willow tree opens vision, communication and it stimulates great dream activity. The best time to attune to it and its energies and spirit is at night.

Exercise:
Meeting the Tree Spirits

1. This exercise is most effective when performed while sitting in the midst of trees, under a tree or in a position to be looking upon the tree itself. Begin your connection with the tree that has always been your favorite. (This reflects that it has

spoken to you already.) If you have no particular favorite, choose a tree that is in your yard or close to your living environment. Because it is in close proximity, you will have already established some kind of connection.

2. Read and explore as much information about the tree as possible. This can be information from a scientific basis or from a mythical/mystical one. The more you understand about the tree, the more you will understand some of the characteristics of its spirit. This will help you in developing resonance with it.

3. If possible, choose a day that is sunny—with little or no breeze. Sit within the tree's shade. The shadow of the tree is a border space that facilitates connecting with the tree spirit and any faeries and elves associated with it. (It is beneficial to think of the tree's shadow as an outward embrace of the tree's spirit.)

   You may wish to sit against the trunk of the tree so that you can feel it. You may want to sit across from it so that you can watch the bark and other tree formations for the appearance of the spirit itself. Choose your position as it suits you at the time. You will find it varies from tree to tree.

4. Close your eyes and take several deep breaths. You may wish to perform a progressive relaxation. The more relaxed you are, the easier it will be to perceive the spirit of the tree itself and others of the faerie realm.

5. In your mind's eye, visualize an image of the tree before you. Its shadow extends toward you, but not quite touching you. See it standing strong and full. The grass beneath you is soft and lush; the air is sweet and clean. The sunlight that penetrates through this tree casts a soft haze around you.

   As you look around, you see you are in a familiar place. It is that small glen that you entered to meet the flower faeries. In the distance is that same high mountain and the path leading up to it. On the opposite of this small glen, the path continues, leading down to the valley below. This is your sanctuary—a place where the real and the imagined meet. It is an intersection of the mortal world and the faerie realm.

The tree stands strong in the midst of this glen—a singular antennae linking the heavens and the Earth. As you look upon it you are thrilled by its simple beauty and strength. With that thought, a soft breeze passes through, rustling the leaves in response. And for a moment you are sure the leaves rustled your name.

You gaze upon the tree and see shadows and movements—tiny flickerings—along the branches and at its base. At first you think it must be squirrels or birds, but you are unable to see them.

As you take in the entire sight of this tree, the lines in the bark begin to change and shift. You can see soft gentle eyes peering out from the bark. You are no longer watching the tree; you are being watched by it.

There is a shadowy movement, and a form steps out from the tree itself to stand in its own shadow. It shimmers and shifts with incredible beauty. Around it flicker several tiny lights, and you know they must be faeries. Peering around from behind it, you see a tiny elfin face, shy but curious. Then the spirit speaks your name. The leaves of the tree rustle again, and you laugh with delight.

As you look upon this being, pay attention to what you experience. Are there specific colors? Fragrances? Do you feel a touch or a tingle on any part of the body? Is this tree spirit male or female? Remember that those of the faerie realm will often use a form they think you expect.

It begins to talk softly to you. It speaks of its purpose and what knowledge it holds. It tells you its role in nature and what role it could serve in your own life. It tells you of the mystery of the tree, and why this one is so important to you.

See this as a conversation between you and the tree. Don't force it. Let the communication flow naturally. Let this being tell you about itself. Let it tell you why it wants to work with you. Don't be afraid to ask questions.

Don't worry that you might be imagining it all and that it's all a product of the mind. You would not be able to imagine it at all if there wasn't something real about it.

The leaves rustle with a singing sound, as this wondrous being speaks. It sends shivers of delight through you. You see specific birds and other wildlife gathering about, and you are told these will be signs of greeting in the future.

It holds its palms upwards, and the shadow of the tree extends further outward, until you are encompassed by it. For the first time, you can actually feel a shadow. Its caress is soft and gentle and loving, and you are filled with a sense of great promise. And then the shadow withdraws.

As it recedes, the eyes of the tree spirit hold yours with tenderness, until the spirit is drawn back into the heart of the tree. You can see its form within the natural configurations of the tree itself, and you know you will forever recognize it from this day forth. The leaves rustle once more, whispering your name, and then they are still.

You feel thrilled and relaxed. And as you do, the scene before you shifts and changes, until you feel yourself sitting where you first began this meditation, comfortable and peaceful. You remember all that you were told, and you now know why you have always been drawn to this tree.

6. At this point breathe deeply and regularly. Listen and feel. Extend your senses out. Do you feel any touches or tingles on any part of the body? Do you hear the whisper of leaves? Do you hear the presence of specific birds or wildlife? Are there any fragrances that stand out?

   Slowly open your eyes, and gaze softly at the tree upon which you were focused for this meditation. Keep a half-focus of the eyes. Do you see any shadows and forms? Can you see the form of the tree spirit within the real tree, just as you did in the meditation?

7. Observe and note anything that you perceive. You may wish to record observations to honor this meeting and future meetings with this tree spirit. Give thanks for the sharing in some way. The old concept of giving a tree a hug is very effective. Touching or hugging the tree will ground your energies, and it will honor the communication and connection with its spirit and those of the faerie realm who call it home.

Chapter Ten

Fantastic Creatures of the Faerie Realm

The animal world, like the faerie realm itself, holds strong appeal to the imagination. Most societies had gods and goddesses who were the guardians and protectors of the animal kingdom. Working with them were many of those of the faerie realm. Even today, many faeries and elves work as guardians to animals.

Although many bestiaries used animals to illustrate moral and religious doctrines (emphasizing the human animal character), the faeries and elves teach us a different aspect of the animal world. Through them, we learn the instinctive altruism of animals and ourselves. By working with the faeries to re-establish relationships with the animal kingdom, we regain our instinctive intuition.

1. We become more sensitive to subtle changes around us. This includes the subtle changes in weather, the seasons, the expressions of others, etc.

2. We learn to read the omens of nature so as to foresee coming events. This is a true future pattern based upon an understanding of animal behavior and not superstition.

3. We learn to recognize and use visual, auditory and tactile signals in communicating with and understanding the world around us—physical and subtle.

4. We learn to recognize the beauty and essence of life in all of its expressions and on all dimensions.

5. We keep our creative imagination strong.

There is so much more to the faerie realm than just faeries, elves, gnomes and elemental spirits. Animals play an integral part. We have talked of the shape-shifting ability of many elves and faeries. The most common forms used are those of animals. The elves and faeries know that the animal world holds strong appeal to the human imagination.

Using an animal form serves several purposes. It enables the faeries and elves to move about without being intruded upon by curious humans. It enables them to observe human behavior without being observed themselves. It is a form that is less intimidating to the average person than many elf and faerie forms. It increases our interest in and fascination for that aspect of Mother Nature. It can also be a form of mischievousness and play.

As we open to the faerie realm, our connection to the animal kingdom will grow. The animals will often appear in unusual relationships with the faerie beings. You might see faeries sitting astride field mice or tiny elves hitching rides upon fireflies. You may see miniature horses and giant birds. And it all serves to break down previous conceptions, while opening us to new perceptions.

You may see a rabbit that is blue, a horse that is red and an eagle that is white. An owl may whisper to you in a foreign accent. You may hear a fly speak on philosophy. You may see a beetle with golden shoes and a fox in coat and tails. A leaf may sing to you as it falls lightly from the tree. A crow may make you laugh until you ache. You may even see the song of the nightingale, like waves of colors upon the air. In the faerie realm the normal becomes fantastic, and the fantastic is all very normal.

When you open to the faeries and elves, you also open to the fantastic creatures that were born of the imagination. This is the home of the mythical beasts and the wondrous animals we have read in our stories and seen in our dreams. Often these wondrous creatures are combinations of the real and the fantastic, but even if only approached from a symbolic level, they help us in transcending normal consciousness and awareness.

You may encounter a winged horse, like Pegasus of Greek mythology. It is a symbol of the heightened power of the natural forces. It reflects the ability to control the animal within us and use its energies to soar to new heights. It can reflect increased ability to move from the mortal world to the faerie realm.

You may even encounter something such as the Norwegian kraken in your explorations of the water element within the faerie realm. This legendary sea monster was the cause of great whirlpools. It had a round, flat body with many arms. It was so large, that sailors often mistook its back for an island. It is a symbol of the mystery of water and the power it has over life.

The fantastic creatures that you may encounter in the faerie realm are just as real as the faeries and elves themselves. They can and should be approached from several perspectives simultaneously. The first is as a life form of its own. Second, they can be viewed as a force of the faerie realm. Its form will reflect how that force is likely to manifest. Third, the creature will always have symbolic significance as well—for you or some aspect of your life.

No matter what the creature is or the form it takes, every aspect of it has significance and should be noted. This includes its color, form, size, temperament, etc. All of these aspects are symbolic and should at least be examined from that perspective in relation to you and your life. The more you understand and find significance in it, the greater its power will manifest for you.

Preconceptions about these mystical and fantastic creatures are often shattered. You may, in fact, encounter a dragon, but it may be the size of a dragonfly. You may encounter a giant or ogre, and find him to be as amiable as your best friend. Remember that connection with the faerie realm helps us to break our limiting perspectives of life and to open to new creative possibilities.

Their energies and their ability to affect you, your consciousness and your life is great. Be careful about making assumptions about them. Dragons are not meant to be slain. They are meant to be controlled as a force that can empower you.

The fantastic creatures of the faerie realm are rare and very reclusive. They show themselves even less readily than the faeries and elves. You may work and play in the faerie realm for years and never even see a shadow of one. In fact, you may never see them at all. If they are encountered though, they will be of great importance and significance to you. It is best not to go in search of them, as their energies are more intense than that of the faeries and elves. It can be extremely difficult to handle. Always keep in mind that—like the elves and faeries—they can be a dynamic catalyst in your life.

The following list is a guideline only. The fantastic creatures of this realm are by no means limited. There are many forms of these and others found in this world.

If you encounter a creature in a fearsome form, it may reflect energies you should be more cautious of in your life. Remember that those of this realm will often use a form that they know you can relate to. It may reflect dangers or that which must be overcome if you are to master walking the threads between the worlds. They can also reflect the power of nature which can be terrifying if not understood and respected.

The list is provided as a guideline only. It will give you some background on the more common creatures that may be encountered and some of their hidden significance and powers. It should help increase your understanding of their role within this realm.

Centaurs

Centaurs are half horse and half human. Most often the half that is human is depicted as male, but there can be a female half. Sometimes the animal half has been depicted as a horse and other times as a wild ass.

In mythology, the centaurs have their origin in Babylonia and originally were guardian spirits. In the Greek tradition, they were considered man-eaters, lecherous and violent.

Creatures with half human and half animal characteristics are very symbolic. They reflect a movement away from the animal. They represent a change in consciousness and a rising to a new plane of awareness.

Centaurs are very sexual creatures, and stimulate strong sexual responses. Encountering one may reflect lessons associated with sexuality and learning to use its dynamic force in new ways. It can symbolize a time of greater knowledge rising out of turbulence.

Encountering a centaur can also signify guardianship in some area of your life. Centaurs occasionally do become patrons of mortals, guiding and teaching them. Chiron is probably the most famous of such patrons. Tutor to Achilles, Hercules and Asclepius, he had great knowledge of medicine, healing and alchemy. Chiron also blessed wedlock.

Weddings are very symbolic alchemical rituals on many levels. They exemplify the reconciliation of opposites, a new union of greater fertility and power. They hold the promise of new life—the promise that is set in motion when one encounters a centaur.

Dragons

Dragons are fantastic creatures which have appeared in various forms throughout the world. Though Christianity has made them out to be evil, they are the epitome of power.

Most dragons have been depicted as composites of other animals. They may have a snake's body and a lion's claws. They may have the wings of an eagle or a bat. They could be multi-headed like the Hydra, or they could shape-shift, using varied forms.

The word "dragon" comes from the Greek "drakon" for serpent or great worm. It was the Greek perception of the dragon that became the prototype for the Western world.

Dragons are often depicted as guarding treasures or doorways to treasures, as in the spring next to the tree upon which hung the Golden Fleece or that which guarded the golden apples of Hesperides. This is often symbolic of hidden wisdom that is going to open up or a new threshold that you will soon cross in your life.

The basilisk was a dragon of great virulence. It is cobra-like and often depicted as a terrifying creature. It breathed fire and had a deadly venom. It could kill with a look from its eyes. If a human encountered a basilisk and laid eyes upon the monster first, the human would live. If the basilisk saw the human first, the human would die.

Many of the qualities of the basilisk and other dragon forms are symbolic. The perception that it could kill probably had as much to do with the shock of seeing something so strange and powerful as it did with the changes that would result in the individual's life and consciousness as a result of such an encounter. The death may reflect a death of some aspect of the individual's life.

As frightening as the basilisk dragon was made to appear, it had great magical properties as well. Its skin could repel snakes and spiders, and silver rubbed with its ashes would become gold. Crystal will reflect its deadly vision and its venom. It has been said that the eyes are the gateways to the soul, and it is through the basilisk form of the dragon that we learn how to read the true soul of individuals by looking into their eyes. This dragon has the knowledge of how to use the eyes to entrance and to control.

The basilisk form of the dragon is one that I invoke and draw into my home environment when I travel. It provides protection for the house and all within it. The energy of this protector is such that those who may think about breaking in, are going to feel very uneasy around the house, so much so that they are more likely to avoid my house entirely.

Other countries had different forms and myths of the dragon. The epitome of the dragon of Old English lore is probably best found in the beast Grendel of the epic Beowulf. In Egypt, the population of serpents, dragons and snakes was controlled by the ibis.

From the Chinese we get a different view of dragons. In Chinese mythology, dragons are powerful, but most often beneficent. Not just traditional fire-breathing beasts, they are associated with each of the elements. There are water dragons and cloud dragons. The imperial dragon (the most powerful) always has five claws and it holds—either in its claws or under its chin—a great pearl. This pearl was magical and could multiply whatever it was placed with—food, money, jewels, whatever.

The dragon has been the source of many creation and destruction myths and tales. If nothing else, this reflects the tremendous power associated with it. It has fired the imagination of people in both the East and West. Of all the creatures in the faerie realm, it is one that still inspires great awe and fear, in spite of its general benevolence.

The dragon comes in many sizes and forms. In most of them, it is the personification of life. Its eyes are often glittering springs or gold. It can see and hear better than almost any creature. Should you encounter a dragon in your explorations of the faerie realm, it may signify that your own senses and life energies will be amplified.

The dragon is the force of wisdom, strength and spiritual power. It is the primal force of creation. It is also the guardian, and when a dragon is encountered you will begin having greater strength and guardianship in your life.

Dragons are wondrous creatures, and one of the great rewards of opening to the faerie realm. As mentioned in Chapter Eight, planting basil (sacred to the basilisk form of dragon) is a means of inviting them into your environment and making yourself more open to their perception.

Giants

Giants have been a part of many creation myths and tales. The Greeks had their Titans and the Teutonic tradition had its own great beings—from frost giants to giant maidens (such as in the tale of Frey and Gerd). In the Sumerian epic of Gilgamesh, the giant Humbaba was the guardian to the garden of Ishtar. And in Biblical scripture we find the tale of the giant Goliath.

Giants are symbols of primeval forces associated with an area of Mother Nature—often guarding some of her treasures. There are hill giants, mountain giants, river giants and forest giants. They reflect and embody the energy of their natural environment. They hold the key to its wisdom and power. They are neither good nor evil, but their energy amplifies that of humans.

Sasquatch (Bigfoot) of North America, the yeti (the abominable snowman) of the Himalayas and other such giant beings are part of the faerie realm. They reflect the energies of the environment and often take a form that enables ease of movement within it. This is why they are so difficult to encounter and verify. Because they are part of the faerie realm, they can take various forms, and they can make themselves visible or invisible.

Giants hold the key to putting things into proper perspective. They also can be a symbol of how best to move beyond your present human stature. The specific characteristics and form of the giant will provide the significant clues.

Giants and great-sized beasts in the faerie realm often serve as tutors and protectors. Although in such stories as *Jack and the Magic Beans* and encounters with the Cyclops in the tale of *Jason and the Argonauts* we see an evil aspect of giants, these are really the exception. For those who don't understand what they are truly encountering in such beings, there will be fear and intimidation. And this is sad, as the giants are incapable of being confined to a specific category.

Giants are an amplification of energies and attitudes, and they will amplify and mirror such back to you. They are drawn to those who need strength, those who are timid and introverted and those who are gentle and childlike. They defend the common folk and the simple nobility of leading a good life.

They will take a form and appearance that is very symbolic and significant to you personally. They are often the guardians of that which should be most treasured, yet is often unrecognized. For example, a one-eyed Cyclops may be a teacher to open the inner eye or to help you develop far-sighted vision.

Mermaids and Mermen

Although discussed earlier in the chapter on spirits of the water element, it also is important to examine these spirits as fantastic creatures of the faerie realm. Mermaids are fair women to the waist with a fishtail below. Sometimes they have two legs, sometimes two tails. They sing beautifully, and are often seen sunning themselves on rocks offshore.

Mermaids are the incarnate beauty of the sights and sounds of water. An encounter with them can enrich or endanger, depending on how well-balanced you are. They will take mortals into their favor, and they are strong and faithful protectors. They are also the guardians and avengers of women.

Mermaids are symbols of tolerance and the separation of the animal from the intellect. They reflect awakening freedom and imagination. They also hold the knowledge of storms and future events, they can grant wishes and can even bestow some supernatural powers. They can reveal treasures and teach wisdom.

Mermen are the male counterparts of mermaids. In Greek mythology, Triton—a sea god born of Poseidon and Amphitrite—was the epitome of this being as he possessed the head and trunk of a man and the tail of a fish.

Sirens

Sirens are often associated with the negative aspects of water spirits. Sometimes they are depicted as bird women, and at other times they are seen as sea nymphs. Traditionally, they were women who sang and played music so sweet and enticing that it lured mariners to destruction on the rocks surrounding their island. In essence, such stories may be more symbolic than anything else, reflecting the enticement of the realm for those who learn to hear its call, and symbolizing the death of one aspect of ourselves as we open to another.

Contact with a siren may bring knowledge of the magical power of words. They hold the knowledge of enchantment and allurement, and though they were often depicted as ugly in appearance, the song that came forth from them made them beautiful. These beings hold the key to finding our own inner beauty—in spite of outer appearances.

Griffin

The griffin has its origin in the Middle East, and it is usually depicted with a combination of animal characteristics. Predominantly, it is part lion and part eagle (the wings and head encompassing the characteristics of the eagle). Others have given it attributes from every part of the animal kingdom: beak of a falcon, eyes of a human, ears of a fish, the tail of a snake, etc. Sometimes it is even depicted with antelope horns to denote its swiftness, and gold feathers upon its head, neck and wings to denote its spiritual magic.

For general discussion, a griffin can be considered any creature that is part mammal and part bird, regardless of the specifics. As bird and beast, it is symbolic of heaven and Earth, spirit and matter, good and evil, guardian and avenger. As guardian, it is considered protective and gentle; as avenger, it is vicious and relentless.

It is often the avenger of the faeries and elves, as it guards their realm against abuse and unwanted intrusion. Such guardianship and protection will take the form of natural phenomena (i.e. storms, etc.). To the Assyrians, the "angel of death" would come in the form of a griffin. It embodies the union between the falcon and its solar aspects and the feline aspects of the night—a symbol of never-ending vigilance.

To encounter a griffin is to encounter great magic and power. It is ever vigilant, and it guards both the Earth and sky. Thus it provides protection while awake and asleep. The griffin has a keen sense of hearing, and when it works as your protector it responds to your softest whisper. It also awakens within you the ability to hear what is behind the words of others.

The griffin is faster than lightning. When first encountered, it is often seen at rest with eyes ever alert. And usually there is thunder and lightning in the background, as if to make it stand out against the sky itself. Generally within three days of a faerie realm encounter with a griffin—no matter how imaginary you may think it may have been—if it was a true encounter, you will see lightning in the sky or there will be a thunderstorm.

After an encounter with a griffin, you will often encounter a feather in the mortal world. It may come as a gift from someone, or you may just happen upon it, but it will be a unique feather. It is usually acquired within seven days. It is a direct link to the griffin and its energies. Holding it and meditating upon it is a way of calling the griffin to you. One of the most beautiful feathers I have ever received came to me after a griffin encounter (related at the end of this chapter).

Eagle, vulture and falcon feathers are directly linked to the griffin of old and were once used in fetishes to attract its influence. The gold eagle particularly, because of the golden feathering around its head and neck, was even more appropriate. (It must be noted that today possession of eagle feathers and the feathers of most raptors is illegal, as many of these species are endangered. Simply possessing an eagle feather can bring a stiff fine and/or imprisonment. They also are not necessary to meeting a griffin in real life.)

Meeting a griffin heralds a time of great power and magic. It lends its immense strength and readiness for whatever task may be at hand. It indicates that a new road is going to open for you soon. When passed over the eyes, its feathers could heal blindness. It signals a time of action and new salvation through linking your psychic energies with your normal day-to-day life activities.

Phoenix

The phoenix is the legendary bird that sacrificed itself to fire and rose renewed from its ashes. Legends and myths contain common threads that link them to the phoenix. The hero lives a long life, and the phoenix appears either just before or after his death. Through death, the hero is able to live again.

With its gold and red feathers, its pheasant-like head and long plumage, the phoenix stirs the body and soul. In Chinese mythology, the plumage is a blending of five colors that have a sweet sound, creating a harmony of five notes. In Egypt, it was linked to the worship of the sun god Ra. Even in Christianity, it is a symbol of the death and resurrection of Jesus.

Traditionally, there is only one phoenix alive at a time, and it lives for five hundred years. It lays a golden egg, and as it is consumed in the fire, the new phoenix breaks out from the egg and rises with the flames. It is an ancient symbol of the sun and of resurrection, life after death. It reflects the immortal soul, love, eternal youth and even self-sufficiency.

It is one of the few fantastic creatures that can be fun to seek. The best time is when the early morning sun is at its peak or when the last of the evening sun can be seen. Spring and autumn are the best times to encounter it. Myrrh is a fragrance that is drawing to it. If encountered, you can expect rebirth within your life. It will always be dynamic and beneficial. It signals a time of new life, energy and a new beginning.

Sphinx

The sphinx is a creature of great mystery. To the Greeks, it was a winged monster having the head of a woman and the body of a lion. In Phoenicia, it had the body of a lion and either a male or fe-male head. To the Egyptians, it was a figure having the body of a lion and the head of a man, ram or hawk. (The latter is more closely connected to the image and power of the griffin, to which the sphinx is related.)

The sphinx was a symbol of divine knowledge, and the power of the mind to raise us to new heights and perceptions. This creature was the guardian of ancient mysteries. To be open to the mysteries, you often had to pass a test or solve a riddle. The penalty for failing was death—often the sphinx itself would devour the individual. In many ways this signifies the danger of knowledge not applied or misused. Forgetfulness, ignorance or any disease of the mind would prevent you from gaining access to the true mysteries and higher wisdom.

Encountering the sphinx indicates a coming period of education, an opportunity for the mind to raise itself above nature. It may indicate that the reason is linked with the soul.

The sphinx has knowledge of the art of prophecy and oracles. It is the keeper of knowledge and beauty of the past and present. It can reveal the potential of any love (good, bad or indifferent). It also holds the key to the physical and spiritual mysteries of intercourse and birth.

Unicorn

The unicorn has become a dynamic symbol of all the magic, enchantment and power of the faerie realm. It has universal appeal and symbolism. It has been written about in India, Africa, China, Mesopotamia, Babylon, early Christianity, and it is even found in modern stories and lore. In Lewis Carroll's *Through the Looking Glass*, Alice encounters a unicorn, and James Thurber wrote of a humorous encounter in his story "The Unicorn in the Garden."

Descriptions of the unicorn vary. To classical writers, the unicorn had a stag's head, the feet of an elephant, the tail of a bear and the body of a horse. It also had a single black horn. Ctesia the Greek, in his work *Indica*, wrote that the unicorn had a white body, a purple head and dark blue eyes. Its horn was white at the base, black in the center and dark red at the tip. Most depictions though give it the form of a horse with a single spiraled horn projecting from its forehead.

Perhaps the greatest reason for the unicorn's widespread appeal is that it falls within the limits of probability. Many animals upon the planet have horns ... so why can't a horse?

The unicorn appeals to the imagination. It is part of the world of dreams. It is a symbol of the sun and long life. It reflects mystery, power, beauty, chastity and ferocity. It is a symbol of humanity's longing for the mysterious and the unattainable. The killing of the unicorn is symbolic of the loss of innocence.

The apple tree is its home, and thus an apple blossom fragrance can be used in meditation to help draw the unicorn out into the open. Cedar is also good, as the unicorn is known to keep its treasures in a cedar box.

Submissiveness, purity of heart and gentle, loving innocence are what draw unicorns out into the open. The search for the unicorn

can be likened to the quest for the Holy Grail—only the strongest and most pure will achieve it.

Encounters with a unicorn can bring new understanding of purity and chastity and the true power of sexuality. The unicorn holds the knowledge and treasures of alchemy. It can stimulate healing, and the unicorn can purify water simply through its presence. More than anything else, an encounter with a unicorn will free the imagination. And when the imagination is truly free, the entire faerie realm is opened wide.

⊱✦⊰

Excerpt From My Personal Journal

While working on the chapter on fantastic creatures for my faerie book, I wondered why a griffin had not come to help while the area behind my house was being torn up. Those beings and creatures of the natural element are always so responsive.

I finished the chapter and noticed that the workers had also finished. It was a sad day. Although they tried to make it look nice, I still felt an aching sense of loneliness.

As I relaxed that evening in front of the TV I heard a loud splintering sound. It sounded much like lightning. I turned down the TV but there was nothing else. Then half an hour later, there was a crash, a splintering and then the house was pitched into darkness. The electricity was out.

I went to the back yard and almost cheered. One of the trees that had been left by the workers had split, as if struck by lightning. The limb fell and wiped out the power lines to the apartment complex and everything within a one-block radius around the area that had been gutted. I couldn't help notice the association of electricity and guardianship of the griffin as it applied to this situation. I closed my eyes and gave a quiet thanks to the griffin that had visited.

The next morning, as I sat on my back porch swing, I spied a small but very unique feather at my feet. As I picked it up, a breeze blew over me. In my mind, I could imagine it as coming from the wings of a griffin. As I held the feather, my body was covered in goose bumps, and I had all the confirmation I needed.

Chapter Eleven

The Blessings of
the Faerie Godmothers

When we begin to explore folktales and myths, we find there have
been many beings of supernatural ability who assisted, guided or
helped change the fate of individuals. In traditional mythologies,
this ability to affect the fate and life of an individual usually fell into
the hands of specific supernatural beings.

Gods and goddesses often had their favorite humans, siding
with them in conflict and providing tools to help them succeed. In
the Greek tale of Perseus, the god Hermes presented him with an in-
vincible sword and information to assist him in his quest. Athena
also lent him her own shield to use as a mirror to be immune to the
gaze of the Medusa.

There were always those who would weave the pattern of life
for men and women. Once woven however, little could be done to
change it, although gods and goddesses would often color the
weaving according to their own fancies. In Greek lore it was the
Fates who controlled the direction of human life: the goddess
Clotho spun the thread of destiny, Lachesis provided the element of
luck, and Atropos governed fatality.

The Scandinavian counterparts to the Greek Fates were the

Norns: Urd (past), Verdandi (present), and Skuld (future). Related to the Norns were the Disir, goddesses of heredity, who controlled an individual's talents and defects. Disir guardians who, in dreams, gave warnings and advice were known as the Hamingjes; the Giptes awarded fortune and treasure to favored humans; and elf maids tended to the unborn and located kind mothers for the infants.

The activities and roles of the Disir fit in closely with the traditional Christian belief in a guardian angel. Every child knows something about guardian angels, and there is a common belief that we are each watched over by one in particular throughout our life. In truth, we are each under the watchfulness of a group of angels (or their younger brothers and sisters of the faerie realm) who assist us without doing for us.

In some societies there are great animal spirits who lend their protection, characteristics and powers to individuals in times of need and testing. This is often found in ancient shamanic cultures, such as those of Native Americans. Sometimes it was an oracle from a spring or well that became the guardian that affected the fate of an individual, and sometimes it was just an old man or woman who was encountered and offered sage advice. In such tales, how that advice is acted upon often determined the future of the tale's hero or heroine.

In yet other instances, simple faeries and elves became temporary and sometimes permanent patrons of humans, for even though many faeries and elves often spend their time fulfilling humble tasks, they do possess extraordinary power. And they often do take a liking to specific humans. This is evidenced in the tale of *The Elves and the Shoemaker*. In the story of *Rumpelstiltskin*, this magical dwarf serves as a temporary patron to the miller's daughter, helping her to spin straw into gold. Of all the tales though, stories such as *Sleeping Beauty*, *Brier Rose* and *Cinderella* truly capture the imagination in regards to faerie godmothers and patrons.

Many in the faerie realm have the ability to bestow great gifts upon mortals. These beings are often called patrons and patronesses, and they protect, guide and help change the fate of both humans and others of the faerie realm. Falling into this category are the traditional faerie godmothers, as well as those faeries and elves who may simply assist us in our normal day-to-day activities.

Those beings which served as inspiration for the faerie godmothers of lore are spirits of great age and power. The white ladies and the fees are the two most common forms of these. With the rise of Christianity and its antagonistic disdain at such beliefs, along with humanity's rationality and its abuses of nature, both had seemed to disappear. They are promised to return in this century, and in my travels I have met people who have had the traditional encounters with them once again.

The white ladies are very ancient and highly evolved. They are actually more along the line of our traditional perception of angels. They usually are only seen when they kiss a child, blessing it , or when you are alone out in nature. When the latter instance occurs, you may simply encounter an old woman strolling through the woods who pauses to greet you. Then when you turn around, you find there is no one there. This is often the first touch and the beginning of the white lady blessing.

The white lady blessing often signals a change in the course and circumstances of your life. What didn't work, will now start. Those things and people which used to cause problems may either correct themselves or disappear from your life. Doors to opportunity begin to open unexpectedly. You begin to meet people more in line with who you are and what you believe.

The fees are often considered the oldest beings upon the planet, and it is from them that we get the traditional image of the faerie godmother with the blue ball gown and magic wand. The color of the gown and its form is actually a representation of the energy that emanates from them. They can be found in every corner of nature. Their advice should always be followed to the letter.

When they borrow something, they always return it with a blessing. In fact their borrowing is one sign of their presence. They appear as strangers who borrow something they know you have on you at the time. The individual is often surprised they could know this. They, like the white ladies, will often disappear—seemingly into thin air—immediately after the borrowing. At some point, what is borrowed is returned, usually without direct contact. You simply come across it by chance, discover another item or amount of money where you least expect it. This is when the blessings begin.

Most faerie patrons and patronesses are beautiful and have great power. They control dynamic elemental force, and they have the respect and love of their younger brothers and sisters. They do not have to be female, as we often assume. As we discussed in the chapter on the fire spirits, those who became the models for the genie of folklore were often patrons. They used a male form most often (though not exclusively), reflecting the dynamic masculine aspect of the fire energy with which they worked.

Some patrons and patronesses align themselves with specific individuals, and others with specific environments. In the latter case, entering into that environment is a way of bringing temporary blessings by the lady of the woods, the lord of the lake, the spirit of the mountain. It is interesting to note that birch groves in particular have a white lady watching over the grove and all who live in it and pass through it. Most of the time she is never directly encountered, but there are those rare occasions.

Most faerie godmothers, patrons and patronesses don't reveal their true appearance or purpose initially. Many societies have tales and myths of individuals who take specific forms to test the charity of human beings that may be potential proteges. Only if the test is passed, will the individual ever have an opportunity to see the patron in true form. If the test is failed, the individual will never know if he or she had missed an opportunity.

In the Hispanic tradition there are tales of the anjana. These beings take the form of old women to test the charity of human beings. If the test is passed, their true form is revealed.

> *In their true form they are beautiful young women, fair haired and blue-eyed, clothed in tunics made of flowers and silver stars. They carry a gold staff and wear green stockings. They watch over animals and have underground palaces of jewels and other treasures. The touch of their staff turns everything into riches.** *

Many societies had stories of guardian spirits and beings who used different forms to test charity. The Bantu people of Africa have many stories of one called Songi, the great mother who appeared as an old woman to protect and to bless. Even the Norse god Odin would walk the world of men in disguise, wearing a hat tilted to cover the hollow of his one eye.

The blessings that were bestowed upon individuals depended greatly on how the patron or patroness was treated in their disguised form. In fact, the patrons and patronesses have specific de-

---

* J. E. Cirlot, *A Dictionary of Symbols*. (New York: Philosophical Library, 1971), p. 13.

mands that must be fulfilled before anyone can become their full protege.

1. The individual must be free.

    This doesn't mean without responsibilities, family, or spouse. It implies a more mental type of freedom. The individual needs to be a free thinker, creative. The individual should not be bound by the structures of societal or religious beliefs.

2. The individual must be open.

    This openness is to new ideas and new possibilities. An inability to look at things anew or from a different perspective will never enable the individual to perceive the faerie realm. The individual must not be bound by the past or the present. This implies a kind of innocence—an childlike innocence that is open and receptive to new wonders.

3. The individual must be generous in dealing with others.

    The ability to be charitable is one of the strongest tests employed by all of those of the faerie realm. This means there should always be a readiness to perform a kindness under any circumstances. Compassion for all forms of life (human, faerie, animal, vegetable, etc.) is an essential aspect of this.

4. The individual must be courteous and hospitable in nature.

    Courtesy is essential in all realms and with all life forms. It is not limited to only humans. This can also be a test that is often used by those of the faerie realm before intimate contact with humans. They will often try to determine just how truly courteous and hospitable you are.

5. The individual must be truthful and straightforward in word and deed.

    As discussed previously, faeries and elves dislike babblers or those who do not take care of their business. Fulfillment of responsibility on all levels is something they hold in high regard. Truthfulness is also extremely essential to them, and they themselves rarely take oaths because of their total disdain of lies. (The idea that lies can only be tolerated and forgiven by the faeries when employed for love or romance has a lot to do with their notorious reputation for amorousness.) A faerie's word or promise is pure, and the expectation from them is that the human word will be the same.

I know of no single method or meditation by which to invite the patronage of someone from this realm. The best means is to simply make yourself available by developing the characteristics listed above. Then spend as much time in nature as possible. Show respect for Mother Nature in all of her manifestations. Involve yourself in creative activities. Sing and meditate in and with the nature realm. Even if it does not bring a faerie godmother into your life, it will surely open for you the whispers of the elves and the caress of the faeries. And this itself will bless your life with wondrous change.

Chapter Twelve

Living the Magical Life

There really is no great mystical secret to living the magical life. It can't be achieved through spells or charms, rituals or incantations. The magical life is not achieved by retreating from life or from the responsibilities of our daily participation in its process. It is being open enough to face the infinite possibilities that exist each day. This can only be accomplished by realizing that growth and maturation do *not* involve denying or ignoring the inner child.

When we were children, the world held for us an ancient enchantment. Each day offered new adventures and new wonders. Everything and everyone was special. Anything we could imagine was real—be it a ghost, a spaceship or even a faerie. We could be anything we wanted. We could be Indians in the morning, be searching out buried treasure in the afternoon and be playing with a unicorn in the evening. There were no limits—no boundaries.

It was a time in which the distance between our world and that which we call imaginary was no further than our closet or back yard. Every blade of grass and every flower had a story to tell. In our search for the modern life, we no longer see with the child's eyes. Instead we scoff and laugh at those who do.

In a world of technology and modern conveniences, we have lost our sensitivity to the nuances of nature. We have built boundaries around our lives and we guard ourselves from that which we don't understand. Though our lives may seem safer, they have also lost much of their wonder.

We have forgotten that there is more to the universe than what abides within the boundaries of our own lives. It is easy to build a false contentment around having a smooth life—no matter how limited or boring. Most people fear going in search for that which may not exist. For many, there will never be any shadow-chasing. "Best to leave well enough alone. Best to be content with what is at hand. Oh, there might be some wonderful things out there somewhere, but there could also be some not-so-wonderful things as well." Such an attitude is sad, for it smothers curiosity and the promise of dreams.

Fear closes the door to the magical life. It silences the streams and it stops the wind. Because of fear, we see animals and plants as things separate from us. Our fears makes us see the only life as human life. Nature is no longer an enchanted world.

Our modern approach to science teaches that every aspect is a secular object or process and not part of an integral whole. Because of this nature has become separated from the sacred. And our ability to feel compassion towards all things upon the Earth has diminished.

We are incarnations of Gaea. We have a personal kinship with things of the Earth—visible and invisible, animate and inanimate. In order to experience this kinship on all levels, we must shift our focus towards the inner. This is difficult though, especially in a world where the primary focus is upon the outer and the superficial, and where we often are living out of proportion.

We must change our perception of ourselves. We must become conscious of ourselves as a walking, breathing, living force. We must see every touch as a passing of power—power to hurt or heal. We must learn to see every word as a tangible stream of energy issuing forth to affect those who hear—to curse or bless. We must learn to see the world through the eyes of each person we meet. We must learn to see each step as an honoring of life and each breath as a prayer. And most importantly, we must realize that our family is not confined to those we grew up with under the same roof.

The one axiom that I hold above all else is: "We are never given a hope, wish or dream without also being given opportunities to make them a reality. And the only thing that can shatter their possibility is compromise." In order to lead a magical life, we must be willing to sacrifice boredom and preconceptions.

By learning to open to the hidden realms of life and their resources, we impact our lives and our environments. We open to our innate ability to work with energy and life at all levels. We learn to align with it, strengthen it and transmute it. Our lives are surrounded and permeated by the awesome power of nature. We have the choice to work with it and create or separate ourselves from it and destroy. The choice is ours.

Those enchanted worlds still exist because the child within us never dies. The doorways may be more obscure, but we can still seek them out. There are still noble adventures to undertake. There are still trees that speak and caverns that lead to nether realms. There will always be faeries and elves dancing within nature because they will always be dancing within our hearts.

❧

May your eyes be always open
May your hearts overflow
That which enchants will also protect—
May this you always know

Music for the Faeries and Elves

INSTRUMENTS DRAWING TO THE NATURE SPIRITS

Gnomes and Earth Spirits

percussion
drums
rattles
gongs
bells
brass

Undines and Water Spirits

chimes
tubulars
strings
singing voice

Sylphs and Air Spirits

wind instruments
flutes
wind chimes

Salamanders and Fire Spirits

sistrum
lyres
harps
composition processes

MUSICAL PIECES THAT INVITE CONTACT WITH THE FAERIE REALM

Richard Wagner

Ride of the Valkyries
Fire Music
Ring of Niebelungs

Edvard Grieg

Hall of the Mountain King
Anitra's Dance
Nocturne

Erik Satie

Gymnopedie

Christoph Gluck

Dance of the Blessed Spirits

Claude Debussy

Nocturnes
The Engulfed Cathedral
Sacred and Profane Dances

Ludwig van Beethoven

Pastoral

Felix Mendelssohn

A Midsummer Night's Dream

Peter Tchaikovsky

Swan Lake
Sleeeping Beauty

Charles Ives

The Pond

Johannes Brahms

Symphony No. 2

~❧~

Appendix B

Astral Doorways to the Faerie Realm

The symbols on the following page are effective in opening the elements of nature from an astral perspective. The symbols are drawn from astrology, and they operate in much the same manner as the Hindu Tattwas* . They open doorways to and activate the associated forces of nature. The symbols are most effective when utilized with the meditations described earlier in the book for connecting with the spirits of each element.

1. After making initial preparations for your meditation (relaxed, undisturbed, etc.), bring your focus upon the two symbols—elemental and spiritual—associated with the element and its spirits with which you wish to connect.

---

* For more information on the Hindu Tattwas, consult *The Golden Dawn* by Israel Regardie (St. Paul, MN: Llewellyn Publications, 1971).

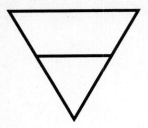

Elemental Earth

Spiritual (Invisible) Earth

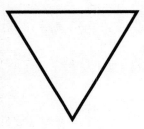

Elemental Water

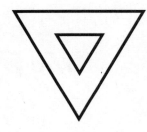

Spiritual (Invisible) Water

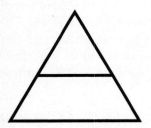

Elemental Air

Spiritual (Invisible) Air

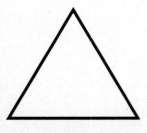

Elemental Fire

Spiritual (Invisible) Fire

2. Study the symbols intently for several minutes so that you will be able to visualize them with your eyes closed. You may wish to visualize them in specific colors to empower their effects.

> earth = earth tones or yellow
> water = green or silver
> air = blue
> fire = red or red-orange

3. Now close your eyes and begin visualizing the elemental symbol. In your mind's eye, see this symbol forming before you as strongly and as clearly as possible. See it growing larger. Visualize and imagine it as a door that you will be able to pass through. The focus upon the elemental symbol activates and calls to the forefront the force and energy of the element.

4. Now visualize yourself stepping through this doorway into a small corridor filled with crystalline white light. You feel safe and protected in this corridor.

5. Now visualize the symbol for the spiritual (invisible) aspect of the same element. See it forming and growing before you to form a second doorway. The focus on this symbol is a signal to those beings of the element with which you want to connect.

6. Now step through this doorway into the meditation or faerie tale you have chosen. Using these two doorways empowers your connection and makes the response to the exercises even more dynamic.

7. At the end of the exercise, step back through the doorway formed by the spiritual (invisible) symbol of the element. Turn and face it, and in your mind's eye, visualize the doorway shrinking and closing. Then turn and step out of this corridor of light through the first doorway formed from the elemental symbol. Visualize the door shrinking and closing and end your meditation.

Bibliography

American Indian Myths and Legends. Ed. by Richard Erdoes and Alfonso Ortiz. New York: Pantheon Books, 1984.

Andrews, Ted. *The Magical Name*. St. Paul, MN: Llewellyn Publications, 1991.

_____. *The Sacred Power in Your Name*. St. Paul, MN: Llewellyn Publications, 1990.

Arnott, Kathleen. *African Myths and Legends*. New York: Oxford University Press, 1979.

Bettelheim, Bruno. *The Uses of Enchantment*. New York: Alfred A. Knopf, Inc., 1976.

Briggs, Katharine. *An Encyclopedia of Fairies*. New York: Pantheon Books, 1976.

British Folktales. Ed. by Katharine Briggs. New York: Dorset Press, 1977.

Clark, Anne. *Beasts and Bawdy*. New York: Taplinger Publications, 1975.

Colum, Padraic. *Treasury of Irish Folklore*. New York: Crown Publications, 1969.

The Complete Fairy Tales of the Brothers Grimm. Trans. by Jack Zipes. New York: Bantam Books, 1987.

The Complete Stories of Hans Christian Andersen. Trans. by H.W. Dulcken. London: Chancellor Press, 1983.

Devas and Men. Wheaton, IL: Theosophical Publishing House, 1977.

Fairies and Elves. Alexandria, VA: Time-Life Books, 1984.

Favorite Folktales from Around the World. Ed. by Jane Yolen. New York: Pantheon Books, 1986.

Hawken, Paul. *The Magic of the Findhorn*. New York: Bantam Books, 1976.

Heslewood, Juliet. *Earth, Air, Fire and Water*. Oxford: Oxford University Press, 1985.

Hildebrandt, Greg. *Favorite Fairy Tales*. New York: Little Simon, 1984.

Hodson, Geoffrey. *Fairies at Work and Play*. Wheaton, IL: Quest Books, 1982.

_____. *Kingdom of the Gods*. Wheaton, IL: Theosophical Publishing House, 1972.

Holiday, Ted and Colin Wilson. *The Goblin Universe*. St. Paul, MN: Llewellyn Publications, 1986.

MacKenzie, Donald A. *German Myths and Legends*. New York: Avenel Books, 1985.

Mythical and Fabulous Creatures. Ed. by Malcolm South. New York: Peter Bedrick Books, 1988.

Stone, Merlin. *Ancient Mirrors of Womanhood*. Boston: Beacon Press, 1979.

Van Gelder, Dora. *The Real World of Fairies*. Wheaton, IL: Quest Books, 1977.

Water Spirits. Alexandria, VA: Time-Life Books, 1985.

Wooton, Anthony. *Animal Folklore, Myth and Legend*. New York: Blandford Press, 1986.

Yeats, W.B. *Treasury of Irish Myth, Legend, and Folklore*. New York: Crown Publications, 1986.

STAY IN TOUCH

On the following pages you will find listed, with their current prices, some of the books now available on related subjects. Your book dealer stocks most of these, and will stock new titles in the Llewellyn series as they become available. We urge your patronage.

To obtain our full catalog, to keep informed of new titles as they are released and to benefit from informative articles and helpful news, you are invited to write for our bimonthly news magazine/catalog, *Llewellyn's New Worlds of Mind and Spirit*. A sample copy is free, and it will continue coming to you at no cost as long as you are an active mail customer. Or you may suscribe for just $10.00 in the U.S.A. and Canada ($20.00 overseas, first class mail). Many bookstores also have *New Worlds* available to their customers. Ask for it.

Stay in touch! In *New Worlds'* pages you will find news and features about new books, tapes and services, announcements of meetings and seminars, articles helpful to our readers, news of authors, products and services, special moneymaking opportunities, and much more.

Llewellyn's New Worlds of Mind and Spirit
P.O. Box 64383-002, St. Paul, MN 55164-0383, U.S.A.

• • •

TO ORDER BOOKS AND TAPES

If your book dealer does not have the books described on the following pages readily available, you may order them directly from the publisher by sending full price in U.S. funds, plus $3.00 for postage and handling for orders *under* $10.00; $4.00 for orders *over* $10.00. There are no postage and handling charges for orders over $50.00. Postage and handling rates are subject to change. We ship UPS whenever possible. Delivery guaranteed. Provide your street address as UPS does not deliver to P.O. Boxes. UPS to Canada requires a $50.00 minimum order. Allow 4-6 weeks for delivery. Orders outside the U.S.A. and Canada: Airmail—add retail price of book; add $5.00 for each non-book item (tapes, etc.); add $1.00 per item for surface mail.

FOR GROUP STUDY AND PURCHASE

Because there is a great deal of interest in group discussion and study of the subject matter of this book, we feel that we should encourage the adoption and use of this particular book by such groups by offering a special quantity price to group leaders or agents.

Our special quantity price for a minimum order of five copies of *Enchantment of the Faerie Realm* is $30.00 cash-with-order. This price includes postage and handling within the United States. Minnesota residents must add 6.5% sales tax. For additional quantities, please order in multiples of five. For Canadian and foreign orders, add postage and handling charges as above. Credit card (VISA, MasterCard, American Express) orders are accepted. Charge card orders only ($15.00 minimum order) may be phoned in free within the the U.S.A. or Canada by dialing 1-800-THE-MOON. For customer service, call 1-612-291-1970. Mail orders to:

LLEWELLYN PUBLICATIONS
P.O. Box 64383-002, St. Paul, MN 55164-0383, U.S.A.

Prices subject to change without notice.

HOW TO MEET & WORK WITH SPIRIT GUIDES
by Ted Andrews

We often experience spirit contact in our lives but fail to recognize it for what it is. Now you can learn to access and attune to beings such as guardian angels, nature spirits and elementals, spirit totems, archangels, gods and goddesses—as well as family and friends after their physical death.

Contact with higher soul energies strengthens the will and enlightens the mind. Through a series of simple exercises, you can safely and gradually increase your awareness of spirits and your ability to identify them. You will learn to develop an intentional and directed contact with any number of spirit beings. Discover meditations to open up your subconscious. Learn which acupressure points effectively stimulate your intuitive faculties. Find out how to form a group for spirit work, use crystal balls, perform automatic writing, attune your aura for spirit contact, use sigils to contact the great archangels and much more!

Read *How to Meet & Work with Spirit Guides* and take your first steps through the corridors of life beyond the physical.

0-87542-008-7, 240 pgs., mass market, illus.   **$3.95**

HOW TO UNCOVER YOUR PAST LIVES
by Ted Andrews

Knowledge of your past lives can be extremely rewarding. It can assist you in opening to new depths within your own psychological makeup. It can provide greater insight into present circumstances with loved ones, career and health. It is also a lot of fun.

Now Ted Andrews shares with you nine different techniques that you can use to access your past lives. Between techniques, Andrews discusses issues such as karma and how it is expressed in your present life, the source of past life information, soul mates and twin souls, proving past lives, the mysteries of birth and death, animals and reincarnation, abortion and pre-mature death, and the role of reincarnation in Christianity.

To explore your past lives, you need only use one or more of the techniques offered. Complete instructions are provided for a safe and easy regression. Learn to dowse to pinpoint the years and places of your lives with great accuracy, make your own self-hypnosis tape, attune to the incoming child during pregnancy, use the Tarot and the Qabala in past life meditations, keep a past life journal and more.

This book will help show that you are master of your own destiny. Your past lives have helped shape and mold you into who you are right now. As this realization increases through uncovering your past lives, your ability to control and reshape your life will also increase. You will become more active within all of life's processes. No longer will you have to bang your head against the wall and cry: "Why is this always happening to me?" This book will assist you in seeing the larger patterns of life within your own individual circumstances.

0-87542-022-2, 224 pgs., mass market, illus.   **$3.95**

Prices subject to change without notice.

HOW TO HEAL WITH COLOR
by Ted Andrews

Now, for perhaps the first time, color therapy is placed within the grasp of the average individual. Anyone can learn to facilitate and accelerate the healing process on all levels with the simple color therapies in *How to Heal with Color*.

Color serves as a vibrational remedy that interacts with the human energy system to stabilize physical, emotional, mental and spiritual conditions. When there is balance, we can more effectively rid ourselves of toxins, negativities and patterns that hinder our life processes.

This book provides color application guidelines that are beneficial for over fifty physical conditions and a wide variety of emotional and mental conditions. Receive simple and tangible instructions for performing "muscle testing" on yourself and others to find the most beneficial colors. Learn how to apply color therapy through touch, projection, breathing, cloth, water and candles. Learn how to use the little known but powerful color-healing system of the mystical Qabala to balance and open the psychic centers. Plus, discover simple techniques for performing long distance healings on others.

0-87542-005-2, 224 pgs., mass market, illus.   **$3.95**

HOW TO SEE & READ THE AURA
by Ted Andrews

Everyone has an aura, the three-dimensional, shape- and color-changing energy field that surrounds all matter. And anyone can learn to see and experience the aura more effectively. There is nothing magical about the process. It simply involves a little understanding, time, practice and perseverance.

Do some people make you feel drained? Do you find some rooms more comfortable and enjoyable to be in? Have you ever been able to sense other people's presences before you actually heard or saw them? If so, you have experienced another person's aura.

In this easy-to-read and practical manual, you receive a variety of exercises to practice alone and with partners to build your skills in aura reading and interpretation. Also, you will learn to balance your aura each day to keep it vibrant and strong so others cannot drain your vital force.

Learning to see the aura not only breaks down old barriers, but it increases sensitivity. As we develop the ability to see and feel the more subtle aspects of life, our intuition unfolds and increases, and the childlike joy and wonder of life returns.

0-87542-013-3, 160 pgs., mass market, illus.   **$3.95**

Prices subject to change without notice.

THE MAGICAL NAME
A Practical Technique for Inner Power
by Ted Andrews

Our name makes a direct link to our soul. It is an "energy" signature that can reveal the soul's potentials, abilities and karma. It is our unique talisman of power. Many upon the spiritual path look for a "magical name" that will trigger a specific play of energies in his or her life.*The Magical Name* explores a variety of techniques for tapping into the esoteric significance of the birth name and for assuming a new, more "magical" name.

This book also demonstrates how we can use the ancient names from mythology to stimulate specific energies in our life and open ourselves to new opportunities. It demonstrates how to use the names of plants, trees and flowers to attune to the archetypal forces of nature. It provides techniques for awakening and empowering the human energy field through working with one's name.

The Magical Name fills a gap in Western magic, which has been deficient in exploring the magic of mantras, sounds and names. It has been said that to hear the angels sing, you must first hear the song within your own heart. It is this song that is echoed within your name!

0-87542-014-1, 360 pgs., 6 x 9, illus.   **$12.95**

THE SACRED POWER IN YOUR NAME
by Ted Andrews

Many seek or wish for some magical incantation that can help them in life, but few realize that when you are born you are given your own individual "magical word." This word can unleash unlimited possibilities within this incarnation. This word is your name.

For those who have no idea where to begin or continue their metaphysical studies, the power and energy inherent in the name is the ideal place to turn. Within our names are the keys to our soul's energies, capabilities and karma. If we come to know and use them properly, we can uncover much about our soul's purpose, growth and potential.

Learn how family karma is reflected through the surname, the dangers and benefits of changing your name, how to transmute your name into a magical incantation, how to heal yourself through your name's tones, how to convert your name to music and discover your "name song."

A large portion of this book consists of a metaphysical dictionary of more than 200 names. Each name listing includes its meaning, a suggested affirmation, the vowel elements in the name, the chakra connected with the vowels, and variations on the name.

0-87542-012-5, 336 pgs., 6 x 9   **$12.95**

SACRED SOUNDS
Transformation Through Music & Word
by Ted Andrews

Everyday we are bombarded by so many energies and forces that it is easy to become unbalanced. One way in which we can learn to restore health and harmony is through the use of rhythms, music and words. Sound has played a key role in magic and mysticism down through the ages and exerts a powerful influence over the mind.

Sacred Sounds in a manual of self-transformation and esoteric healing through the use of simple sound and toning techniques. On a physical level, these techniques have been used to alleviate aches and pains of all kinds, balance hyperactivity in children and lower blood pressure. On a metaphysical level, they have been used to induce altered states of consciousness, open new levels of awareness, stimulate intuition and increase creativity.

In this book, Ted Andrews reveals the magical and healing aspects of resonance and music, the tones and instruments that affect the chakras, the use of kinesiology and "muscle testing" in relation to sound responses, techniques for using musical astrology, the healing aspects of vocal tones, how to use mystical words of power, the art of magical storytelling, how to create prayer-poems, how to write magical quatrains and sonnets, how to form healing groups and utilize group toning for healing and enlightenment, and much more.

0-87542-018-4, 232 pgs., 5-1/4 x 8, illus.   **$7.95**

MAGICKAL DANCE
Your Body as an Instrument of Power
by Ted Andrews

Choreograph your own evolution through one of the most powerful forms of magickal ritual: dance. When you let your inner spirit express itself through movement, you can fire your vitality, revive depleted energies, awaken individual creativity and transcend your usual perceptions.

Directed physical movement creates electrical changes in the body that create shifts in consciousness. It links the hemispheres of the brain, joining the rational and the intuitive to create balance, healing, strength and psychic energy.

This book describes and illustrates over twenty dance and other magickal movements and postures. Learn to shapeshift through dance, dance your prayers into manifestation, align with the planets through movement, activate and raise the kundalini, achieve group harmony and power, and much more.

Anyone who can move any part of the body can perform magickal movement. No formal dance training is required.

0-87542-004-4, 240 pgs., 6 x 9, photographs, illus.   **$9.95**

Prices subject to change without notice.

IMAGICK
Qabalistic Pathworking for Imaginative Magicians
by Ted Andrews

The Qabala is rich in spiritual, mystical and magical symbols. These symbols are like physical tools, and when you learn to use them correctly, you can construct a bridge to reach the energy of other planes. The secret lies in merging the outer world with inner energies, creating a flow that augments and enhances all aspects of life.

Imagick explains effective techniques of bridging the outer and inner worlds through visualization, gesture, and dance. It is a synthesis of yoga, sacred dance and Qabalistic magick that can enhance creativity, personal power, and mental and physical fitness.

This is one of the most personal magickal books ever published, one that goes far beyond the "canned" advice other books on Pathworking give you.

0-87542-016-8, 312 pgs., 6 x 9, illus.   **$12.95**

SIMPLIFIED MAGIC
A Beginner's Guide to the New Age Qabala
by Ted Andrews

In every person, the qualities essential for accelerating his or her growth and spiritual evolution are innate, but even those who recognize such potentials need an effective means of releasing them. The ancient and mystical Qabala is that means.

A person does not need to become a dedicated Qabalist in order to acquire benefits from the Qabala. *Simplified Magic* offers a simple understanding of what the Qabala is and how it operates. It provides practical methods and techniques so that the energies and forces within the system and within ourselves can be experienced in a manner that enhances growth and releases our greater potential. *A reader knowing absolutely nothing about the Qabala could apply the methods in this book with noticeable success!*

The Qabala is more than just some theory for ceremonial magicians. It is a system for personal attainment and magic that anyone can learn and put to use in his or her life. The secret is that the main glyph of the Qabala, the Tree of Life, is *within* you. The Tree of Life is a map to the levels of consciousness, power and magic that are within. By learning the Qabala you will be able to tap into these levels and bring peace, healing, power, love, light and magic into your life.

0-87542-015-X, 208 pgs., mass market, illus.   **$3.95**

DREAM ALCHEMY
Shaping Our Dreams to Transform Our Lives
by Ted Andrews

What humanity is rediscovering is that what we dream can become real. Learning to shift the dream to reality and the reality to dream—to walk the thread of life between the worlds—to become a shapeshifter, a dreamwalker, is available to all. We have the potential to stimulate dream awareness for greater insight and fulfillment.

Through the use of our ancient myths and tales, we can initiate a process of dream alchemy. Through control of the dream state and its energies, we are put in touch with realities and energies that can open us to greater productivity during our waking hours.

For those just opening to the psychic and spiritual realms, this is one of the safest and easiest ways to bridge your consciousness to higher realms. No tools are necessary. It costs nothing—only limited waking time and persistence. These two, when used with the techniques in this book, will stimulate greater dream activity, lucid dreaming, higher inspiration and ultimately even controlled out-of-body experiences. It is all part of the alchemical process of the soul!

0-87542-017-6, 280 pgs., 6 x 9, illus.   **$12.95**

DREAMS AND WHAT THEY MEAN TO YOU
by Migene Gonzalez-Wippler

Everyone dreams. Yet dreams are rarely taken seriously—they seem to be only a bizarre series of amusing or disturbing images that the mind creates for no particular purpose. Yet dreams, through a language of their own, contain essential information about ourselves which, if properly analyzed and understood, can change our lives. In this fascinating and well-written book, the author gives you all of the information needed to begin interpreting—even creating—your own dreams.

Dreams and What They Mean to You begins by exploring the nature of the human mind and consciousness, then discusses the results of the most recent scientific research on sleep and dreams. The author analyzes different types of dreams—telepathic, nightmares, sexual and prophetic. In addition, there is an extensive Dream Dictionary which lists the meanings for a wide variety of dream images.

Most importantly, Gonzalez-Wippler tells you how to practice creative dreaming—consciously controlling dreams as you sleep. Once you learn to control your dreams, your horizons will expand and your chances of success will increase a hundredfold!

0-87542-288-8, 240 pgs., mass market   **$3.95**

Prices subject to change without notice.

HOW TO MAKE AND USE A MAGIC MIRROR
Psychic Windows Into New Worlds
by Donald Tyson

Author Donald Tyson takes the reader step-by-step through the creation of this powerful mystical tool. You will learn about:

- Tools and supplies needed to create the mirror
- Construction techniques
- How to use the mirror for scrying (divination)
- How to communicate with spirits
- How to use the mirror for astral travel

Tyson also presents a history of mirror lore in magic and literature. For anyone wanting their personal magical tool, *How to Make and Use a Magic Mirror* is a must.
0-87542-831-2, 176 pgs., mass market, illus. **$3.95**

CELTIC MAGIC
by D. J. Conway

Many people, not all of Irish descent, have a great interest in the ancient Celts and the Celtic pantheon, and *Celtic Magic* is the map they need for exploring this ancient and fascinating magical culture.

Celtic Magic is for the reader who is either a beginner or intermediate in the field of magic, providing an extensive "how-to" of practical spellworking. There are many books on the market dealing with the Celts and their beliefs, but none guide the reader to a practical application of magical knowledge for use in everyday life. There is also an in-depth discussion of Celtic deities and the Celtic way of life and worship, so that an intermediate practitioner can expand upon the spellwork to build a series of magical rituals.

Presented in an easy-to-understand format, *Celtic Magic* is for anyone searching for new spells that can be worked immediately, without elaborate or rare materials, and with minimal time and preparation.
0-87542-136-9, 240 pgs., mass market, illus. **$3.95**

NORSE MAGIC
by D. J. Conway

The Norse—adventurous Viking wanderers, daring warriors, worshipers of the Aesir and the Vanir. Like the Celtic tribes, the Northmen had strong ties with the Earth and Elements, the Gods and the "little people."

Norse Magic is an active magic, only for participants, not bystanders. It is a magic of pride in oneself and the courage to face whatever comes. It interests those who believe in shaping their own future, those who believe that practicing spellwork is preferable to sitting around passively waiting for changes to come.

The book leads the beginner step by step through the spells. The in-depth discussion of Norse deities and the Norse way of life and worship set the intermediate student on the path to developing his or her own active rituals.

Norse Magic is a compelling and easy-to-read introduction to the Norse religion and Teutonic mythology. The magical techniques are refreshingly direct and simple, with a strong feminine and goddess orientation.
0-87542-137-7, 240 pgs., mass market, illus. **$3.95**

Prices subject to change without notice.

THE 21 LESSONS OF MERLYN
A Study in Druid Magic & Lore
by Douglas Monroe

For those with an inner drive to touch genuine Druidism—or who are fascinated by the lore of King Arthur—*The 21 Lessons of Merlyn* will come as a welcome adventure into history and magic. This is a complete introductory course in Celtic Druidism, packaged within the framework of 21 authentic and expanded folk story/lessons that read like a novel. These lessons, set in late Celtic Britain ca A.D. 500, depict the training and initiation of the real King Arthur at the hands of the real Merlyn-the-Druid: one of the last great champions of Paganism within the dawning age of Christianity.

As you follow the boy Arthur's apprenticeship from his first encounter with Merlyn in the woods, you can study your own program of Druid apprenticeship with the detailed practical ritual applications that follow each story. The 21 folk tales were collected by the author in Britain and Wales during a ten-year period; the Druidic applications come from an unpublished 16th-century manuscript entitled *The Book of Pheryllt*.

0-87542-496-1, 448 pgs., 6 x 9, photographs, illus.   **$12.95**

THE BOOK OF GODDESSES & HEROINES
by Patricia Monaghan

The Book of Goddesses & Heroines is a historical landmark, a must for everyone interested in Goddesses and Goddess worship. It is not an effort to trivialize the beliefs of matriarchal cultures. It is not a collection of Goddess descriptions penned by biased male historians throughout the ages. It is the complete, non-biased account of Goddesses of every cultural and geographic area, including African, Japanese, Korean, Persian, Australian, Pacific, Latin American, British, Irish, Scottish, Welsh, Chinese, Greek, Icelandic, Italian, Finnish, German, Scandinavian, Indian, Tibetan, Mesopotamian, North American, Semitic and Slavic Goddesses!

Unlike some of the male historians before her, Patricia Monaghan eliminates as much bias as possible from her Goddess stories. Envisioning herself as a woman who might have revered each of these Goddesses, she has done away with language that referred to the deities in relation to their male counterparts, as well as with culturally relative terms such as "married" or "fertility cult." The beliefs of the cultures and the attributes of the Goddesses have been left intact.

Plus, this book has a new, complete index. If you are more concerned about finding a Goddess of war than you are a Goddess of a given country, this index will lead you to the right page. This is especially useful for anyone seeking to do Goddess rituals. Your work will be twice as efficient and effective with this detailed and easy-to-use book.

0-87542-573-9, 456 pgs., 6 x 9, photographs   **$17.95**

Prices subject to change without notice.

EARTH POWER
Techniques of Natural Magic
by Scott Cunningham

Magic is the art of working with the forces of Nature to bring about necessary, and desired, changes. The forces of Nature—expressed through Earth, Air, Fire and Water—are our "spiritual ancestors" who paved the way for our emergence from the pre-historic seas of creation. Attuning to, and working with these energies in magic not only lends you the power to affect changes in your life, it also allows you to sense your own place in the larger scheme of Nature. Using the "Old Ways" enables you to live a better life, and to deepen your understanding of the world about you.

The tools and powers of magic are around you, waiting to be grasped and utilized. This book gives you the means to put magic into your life, shows you how to make and use the tools, and gives you spells for every purpose.

0-87542-121-0, 176 pgs., 5-1/4 x 8, illus. $8.95

EARTH, AIR, FIRE & WATER
More Techniques of Natural Magic
by Scott Cunningham

A water-smoothed stone. The wind. A candle's flame. A pool of water. These are the age-old tools of natural magic. Born of the Earth, possessing inner power, they await only our touch and intention to bring them to life.

The four Elements are the ancient powerhouses of magic: Earth for money and employment, Air for intelligence and travel, Fire for protection and courage, and Water for love and healing. Using their energies, we can transform ourselves, our lives and our worlds through the natural, positive practice of magic.

Earth, Air, Fire & Water is a continuation of Scott Cunningham's wildly successful *Earth Power: Techniques of Natural Magic*. Readers of *Earth Power* wanted more: more rites, spells and simple rituals that they could do with a minimum of equipment.

Here, then, is more. Readers will discover the wonders of star magic; the uses of candles, magnets, ice and snow; even the fine art of using wishing wells. This book also looks at the magical properties of the ocean, mirrors and stones, as well as a unique look at "Time Magic." The last chapter is a step-by-step, detailed guide to designing your own magical rituals and spells for any goal you desire.

0-87542-131-8, 240 pgs., 5-1/4 x 8, illus. $9.95

Prices subject to change without notice.